STILL THE ONE

Ally Fletcher fights her way through a torrential downpour to Mr Burke Winslow and his bride at their marriage ceremony! Ally's arrival at the church halts the nuptials when she delivers her bombshell: the groom is already married — to her! However, this businessman isn't in love: he needs a wife for two weeks, purely for financial reasons. Anyone will do — even his insufferable ex. Soon Burke and Ally are temporarily reliving their disastrous marriage — and their sensational, sizzling honey-moon . . .

Books by Joan Reeves
in the Linford Romance Library:

LOVE WILL FIND A WAY
MOST WANTED
SAY YES

JOAN REEVES

STILL
THE ONE

Complete and Unabridged

LINFORD
Leicester

First published in
the United States of America in 1999

First Linford Edition
published 2009

British Library CIP Data

Reeves, Joan
    Still the one.—Large print ed.—
    Linford romance library
    1. Love stories
    2. Large type books
    I. Title
    823.9'2 [F]

    ISBN 978–1–84782–606–0

Published by
F. A. Thorpe (Publishing)
Anstey, Leicestershire

Set by Words & Graphics Ltd.
Anstey, Leicestershire
Printed and bound in Great Britain by
T. J. International Ltd., Padstow, Cornwall

This book is printed on acid-free paper

This is for Micky Chamberlain
Reeves, who possesses the finest
attributes of any hero who ever
graced the pages of a novel.
Thank you, Micky, for
enriching my life.
I couldn't imagine my
world without you.

And, as always, for L. A. R.
Thanks for the memories!

1

Ally Fletcher had waited six years — six long years — for this opportunity. There was no way a mere thunderstorm was going to stop her.

She peered anxiously through the river of rain that washed down the windshield, watching for the church. The sluggish wipers just couldn't keep pace with a downpour that reduced visibility to zero.

A mere thunderstorm? That was like saying a Texas tornado was a mere puff of wind, Ally thought, worried that she might miss the old limestone block building.

Suddenly, the church loomed out of the early evening fog and Ally slammed on the brakes. She jerked the steering wheel of the rental car sharply to the right in an effort to execute the turn into the parking lot. Big mistake.

The little blue car spun in a circle, and only stopped when it smashed into a sleek black Jaguar parked along the driveway. She didn't even have time to scream, but the impact jarred Ally from the top of her too-tight chignon to the toes of her black patent pumps.

The rental car shuddered, then wheezed and died. Ally released the breath that had caught somewhere between her lungs and her throat. This was the perfect ending to a perfectly horrible day.

With shaking hands, she shoved the gear shift into low and yanked up the parking brake. She didn't have time to waste on hysterics. Her flight from Dallas Love Field had landed thirty minutes late at Houston Hobby Airport due to the storm.

Desperate to get to the small town of Brookwood, fifteen miles southeast of Houston, she had taken the only available car at the rental agency — even though that meant contorting her five feet seven inches into a car obviously engineered for one of the smaller inhabitants of Munchkin Land.

Belatedly, the clerk at the rental car counter had warned her that the car's air conditioner was a little tricky. She'd soon found out that it didn't work at all.

Somehow, she'd negotiated Houston's flooded streets and in record time — for rush hour traffic, anyway — she'd reached her exit.

By the time Ally had turned onto the two-lane road leading to Brookwood, the rainy June evening had become a steamy experience in the confines of a car that was about as roomy as a tunafish can. The tricky air conditioner had cooperated with Houston's humidity to melt her carefully applied makeup. And now this!

Disgusted, Ally smacked the steering wheel with her palms. She'd just leave the darn car where it was — right front fender smack dab up against the left rear fender of the Jag. She'd take care of this problem, and the sure-to-be irate owner of the Jag, later.

Ally yanked the door handle upward. The door didn't budge. She groaned. She didn't have time for this. Exasperated, she pulled hard and shoved with her shoulder. The door flew open. With a startled cry, Ally fell out into the rain.

Instinctively, she broke her fall with her hands, earning herself two abraded palms for her efforts. Really angry now — at the lousy car, the rain that drenched her, the rush hour traffic, and the phone call that had started this insanity — she scrambled to her feet. Impulsively, she kicked the offending door with her right foot.

'Owww!' She yelped in pain, but the door stayed shut. Hopping on her left foot, she moaned, 'Can this get any worse?'

This was all Burke's fault. She hadn't seen the blasted man in six years. Six years of a quiet, orderly life. But from the moment her grandmother had mentioned his name this afternoon, her world had begun to tip crazily on its axis.

'You're going to pay for this, Burke Winslow!' she muttered, shivering in the pouring rain. Limping, she dashed to the church steps, wincing with pain each time her sore right foot touched the pavement.

The expensive black sheath dress she wore offered no protection from the weather. She thought longingly of the matching jacket, lost somewhere during the mad dash from Dallas to Houston. The disappearance of the expensive raw silk jacket was another reason to hate Burke Winslow.

When she'd conceived this plan, Ally had pictured herself arriving at the church and looking as if she'd stepped off the pages of *Vogue*. Instead, she probably looked like a newspaper photograph of someone who'd been caught in a mudslide.

With her foot throbbing and rain dripping from her hair, she shoved open the iron-hinged double doors of the church.

She'd wanted to look sophisticated

and gorgeous in her best outfit. On the plane, she'd envisioned herself strolling down the center aisle of the church, with every man's eyes on her. Especially Burke's intense hazel eyes. In her daydream, she'd been calm and collected, and oh, so cool. Well, she was cool, all right, she thought, teeth chattering.

For a moment, Ally considered abandoning her impulsive plan. But maybe, she rationalized, she didn't look as bad as she thought. The moment of sanity flitted by.

When this was over, Ally decided, she was going to have a nice nervous breakdown. But right now, she just didn't have the time. The wedding had probably already started.

2

Burke Winslow had a knot the size of a hockey puck in his gut. At least it had started in his gut. As soon as the minister had said, 'Dearly beloved,' the hockey puck had migrated upward. Now, it seemed to be lodged in his throat.

He swallowed. The stiffly-starched white collar encircling his neck made no allowance for a hockey puck. He could hardly breathe. He looked around, not hearing a word the minister was saying. As if in a dream, he noted the baskets of ferns and orange-speckled lilies that flanked the altar.

Three women wearing satin dresses the color of orange sherbet looked distinctly uncomfortable in their puff-sleeved, bell-skirted concoctions. He'd overheard one of the bridesmaids grumble that brides always picked hideous colors and unflattering styles for their attendants so that the bride, by contrast, would appear even more beautiful.

That could be the only justification for the choices made by Tiffany, his business partner. No, he corrected himself. Today she was more than his cut-throat, cut-to-the-chase partner. She was his bride. At least in name only.

His bride? A drumbeat began pounding in his temples. Even if in name only, the thought made a shudder of apprehension sweep through him.

Burke glanced to his right. His brother Rod, the best man, and Burke's two best friends, Dave Hernandez and Craig Bishop, groomsmen, stood there, looking far more comfortable in their tuxedos than Burke felt in his, though judging by their expressions you'd think they were pallbearers at a funeral instead of attendants at a wedding.

His eyes swung back to Tiffany. It was as if he were watching his life flash before his eyes. Suddenly, he wondered what on earth he was doing. Was any business deal worth marrying a woman you didn't love? Sure, old Tiff was a great business partner. She'd helped their company grow to its present financial stature, but that was no reason to make her his wife. Burke felt a primal instinct to flee. His feet shuffled restlessly.

'What are you doing?' Tiffany hissed.

Burke looked at her and felt as if he were seeing the real Tiffany for the first time. She looked extremely displeased. Odd. He'd never noticed those frown lines between her eyes. True, they were faint, but he could see how they'd be deeply cut in a few years.

In fact, the more he studied the lines, the more they seemed like furrows carved into her skin. Now that he thought about it, Tiffany did frown quite a bit. He'd never realized that before. Just like he'd never known she had such bad taste. His eyes swung back to the orange sherbet bridesmaids' dresses.

Tiffany's green eyes narrowed. Usually, he appreciated that focused stare because it meant she was calculating some strategy that would increase the company's profits. That was one thing he really liked about Tiff, she was all business. Today, however, that shrewd look gave him a definite chill.

'Burke Winslow, don't you dare embarrass me. Now is not the time to get cold feet!'

Burke swallowed hard and almost audibly. Her words sounded like the warning hiss from a snake. Not like the sexy whisper a bride should use. And the way she seemed to read his mind was positively scary.

'We agreed this was the thing to do. Remember?' she hissed again.

We didn't agree, he wanted to shout. She had conceived this hare-brained plan and had talked him into it. And she sure hadn't hissed when she'd been persuading him to do this. He just couldn't marry a woman that hissed — even if it was to be a marriage in name only.

Beads of sweat popped out on his forehead. Suddenly, Burke was certain that he was making the biggest mistake of his life. No, he corrected himself, the second biggest. The honor of biggest mistake had already been awarded to his first marriage fiasco.

Panicked, he decided that he had to stop this farce before it went any further. But how? Tiffany had a lot of pride. She might be a pain in the neck sometimes, but she was his partner. He sighed. More importantly, she was a friend. And even if she weren't, he wasn't about to do something utterly undignified, like walk out.

Old Tiff had dignity up to her eyeballs, and a stiff-necked unyielding pride. Injuring that pride would be as foolhardy as waving a red flag in front of a Texas Longhorn — and the consequences might be just as dire.

She'd be homicidal if he suddenly called the wedding off — from the altar! Burke felt sick. The nauseous feeling gave him immediate inspiration. They'd

11

have to cancel the ceremony if he suddenly tossed his cookies, wouldn't they?

'Burke Winslow!' Tiffany hissed again. 'This is the answer to our problem. Remember?'

Her words forced cold reality to counter the emotion that threatened him. He was wedged between a rock and a hard place. With a sigh, he acknowledged that everything had progressed too far. Like a doomed aircraft, they'd passed the point of no return. He'd have to go through with this insanity.

'Yeah, I remember,' he muttered for her ears alone. 'But *this* was your idea, and I was just fool enough to let you convince me it would work.' And in that moment, he knew he couldn't go through with it. It just wasn't right.

He cleared his throat and prepared to speak up. Tiffany might not have a life outside of business. He'd always thought it strange that such a gorgeous woman was completely oblivious when it came to men. Why, he'd be surprised if she ever had a date. But he had a social life. Didn't he?

Burke frowned and tried to remember his last date. When he drew a total blank, he realized that he and Tiffany were two of a kind. Maybe they did deserve each other. He suspected that no one else would want two workaholics like them.

'No, Burke!' Tiffany swayed against him and ground her satin-slippered foot into his instep.

Burke grimaced in pain.

'Don't you dare back out,' Tiffany whispered. 'You agreed, and I'm holding you to it.'

Burke swallowed an exclamation of pain and looked into her eyes. Even as panicked as he was, he recognized the warning emanating like laser rays from her big green eyes.

'Okay, okay,' he muttered to her. She rewarded him with a pleased smile. She was right. He had agreed with Tiffany that they'd worked too hard to pass up this opportunity. She had come up with an ingenious way around a sticky situation. And it wasn't as if he had to romance Tiff. They'd both laughed at that idea.

Resigned to his fate, Burke shrugged. He'd survived one marital breakup. Kind of. He could do it again. At least he wasn't deluding himself that he and Tiffany were madly in love. This wouldn't be bad at all compared to his first marriage and divorce.

He heard the minister solemnly intone, 'If anyone here knows why this man and this woman should not be joined in holy wedlock, let him speak now or — '

'Stop the wedding!' a woman's voice rang out.

Burke rolled his eyes heavenward and murmured a fervent, 'Thank you.' Sweet relief swept away his desperation the way sunshine chased away dark clouds.

Tiffany elbowed him sharply and hissed a word that should never be said in church. Though he felt like laughing aloud, Burke assumed a poker face. He was saved. Despite his rationalizations only moments before, he could only rejoice as he turned to view his salvation.

A soft chorus of gasps and whispers swept the church. Someone giggled nervously. Everyone craned their necks to see who had shouted the objection.

A woman limped from the back of the sanctuary. Each step she took squished wetly and left a muddy footprint on the rich amethyst carpet. Even at this distance, she looked oddly familiar.

Her rain-soaked hair clung to her head in a drooping knot that seemed to have lost its mooring. It hung precariously above her right ear at the moment while the rest of her hair seemed to be plastered to her forehead. Rain dripped from the hem of her dress. In all, she was the embodiment of the old cliché — she really did look like something the cat had dragged in.

'What's the meaning of this?' Tiffany demanded. Crimson stained each sculpted cheekbone. Then she turned on him. 'Is this your idea of a joke?' Her narrowed eyes, like chips of green glass, were ablaze with anger.

'No. Of course not. Why would I do something like this? You know I need this marriage.' And he did. He needed it. He breathed deeply, nearly weak with relief. He might need a wife, but he sure didn't want one.

Sheepishly, he looked over at Tiffany, knowing he wasn't going to proceed with the wedding since he'd been granted a reprieve in the form of this bedraggled mystery woman. Whoever she was, she was the answer to his desperate prayer.

Somehow, he'd make it up to Tiffany, he decided, unable to feel any regret. Downright cheerful, he planned how he'd explain it. He'd liken it to a business deal that had fallen through. Old Tiff would understand. She had to because nothing on earth could make him marry her now. He rocked back on his heels, relieved at this turn of events.

'Please wait, I can explain,' the woman called out. A new round of mutters swept the church.

Burke's smile faltered. He frowned. That voice! His brows rose and his eyes widened. He straightened and focused his full attention on the woman.

It couldn't be.

He watched as she closed the distance between them. The rain had ruined her hairstyle — and her shoes — but it had done wonders for her plain dress, one of those black numbers women like to fill their closets with. The drenching it had received molded it to a ripe body lushly curved in all the right places.

His eyes flew to the woman's face.

It was!

Beneath the sodden, straggling hair, was the living, breathing proof of the biggest mistake in his life — his ex-wife, Ally Fletcher.

3

'You!'

All Burke's defenses went on red alert. Adrenalin rushed through his veins. If it were a choice of fight or flight, he'd definitely pick the former. A dizzying whirl of emotions overloaded his senses as he tried to figure out how Ally could have shown up at this time and this place.

Relief gave way to a dazed joy. In an instant, that heated up to a fiery anger that burned away all other emotions, leaving Burke with white hot outrage amidst the six-year-old ashes of pain.

How dare Ally burst in here like this and ruin his wedding? He ignored the small voice inside his head that reminded him of his own reluctance to marry Tiffany.

Burke's anger at Ally's sudden reappearance, here and now, grew with each step she took. Did she think she could just rush into his life and he'd welcome her back to his world with open arms? Well, she had another think coming. He crossed his arms. His jaw hardened with resolve. He'd be delighted to show Ally Fletcher just how over her he was.

He'd fantasized for years about giving her a dose of her own medicine. How would she like a great big spoonful of heartbreak? His eyes narrowed on her face.

Nothing would stop him from marrying Tiffany now, he vowed, especially if it was something Ally objected to. He smiled grimly and waited for his ex-wife to speak.

Burke's forbidding expression made Ally wish that she had handled things differently. She'd been crazy to fly down here. She should have called despite Granny Edith's objections. Even a singing telegram would have been preferable to facing him in front of all these people.

Ally felt dizzy as she looked into Burke's hazel eyes. Oh! She remembered those eyes only too well. Once, they'd gazed at her with hot passion. Now, those eyes looked as hard and lethal as stone arrowheads.

'Burke, let me explain,' Ally said. She tried to brush the wet tendrils of hair from her forehead as she gathered her courage, but the mixture of rain and hairspray held the strands to her face as securely as nail glue. In that moment, she felt as ugly as when she'd been a chubby child. She fought the feelings of insecurity those memories brought.

'Burke, get her out of here so we can get on with this,' Tiffany demanded.

Ally's icy stare could have chilled a martini as she contemplated Burke's bride. Ally disliked her on sight. She was exactly the type that Burke had always liked — a petite, blond Barbie clone with a chest measurement greater than her IQ.

'I would like to speak to you,' Ally said, ignoring the woman. 'Privately, please,' she added, determined to be rational and calm.

'Just go away, whoever you are,' Tiffany barked.

Ally looked her up and down. She disliked everything about the woman, from her flawless peaches-and-cream complexion to her tiny feet encased in rhinestone-trimmed white satin heels.

How dare Burke's bride look so pristine and perfect after the day to which Ally had been subjected? That made Ally's dislike deepen.

'What kind of stunt are you pulling, Ally?'

Ally glared at him. 'This is not easy, Burke. Please?'

'Easy? When did you ever make it easy on me?'

Burke's lips thinned. He braced his fists on his hips and faced the woman who had once melted his heart enough for him to marry her. Even muddy and bedraggled, she still twisted his insides into knots. Ruthlessly, he shoved his burgeoning desire away. He was crazy to entertain thoughts like that.

'I didn't come here to rehash the past,' she said. A murmur from the crowd made her look over her shoulder.

Burke realized the exact moment when she discovered that a hundred people were hanging on her every word. He eyed her rising blush with satisfaction.

'This better be good. What the h — ' Burke remembered where he was, 'heck are you doing here?' He crossed his arms and tapped his right foot impatiently.

The tapping reminded Ally of a ticking clock — on a time bomb. She gulped, acutely aware of the rashness of her actions since Granny had told her that Burke was getting married tonight.

What had possessed her? If he was this upset with her for stopping the wedding, she didn't want to be within five miles of him when he discovered the reason why she'd interrupted the ceremony. He wasn't going to be a happy camper.

'Ally?' His questioning voice held a note of warning.

She stalled. Her gaze swept the small crowd. She recognized several of the guests. They had attended her wedding to Burke in this same church. The memory was bittersweet — heavy on the bitter.

Burke's grandfather sat on the groom's side of the church, just as he had during her own wedding to Burke. To her surprise, he winked at her. Ally managed a weak smile and nodded. She'd always liked Frederick Winslow.

'Focus, Ally,' Burke taunted. 'Concentrate. What do you want?'

'Want?' Her eyes flew to Burke's face. Even if he hadn't been standing three steps above her, he would still have towered over her by five inches. She would not acknowledge the desire that made her toes curl when she looked at him. She wouldn't, she vowed silently.

Now twenty-eight, Burke was even more gorgeous than when she'd married him. His shock of sandy hair was still thick and full. A few faint lines gave his face character and made him more appealing than ever. What did she want? Oh, baby!

'Ally!' Burke demanded sharply.

'Yes, well,' she said, horrified at how breathless she sounded. Her mouth snapped closed. She suppressed her unexpected physical response to him. Don't even go down that road, she chided herself. But she couldn't stop the shiver that coiled up her spine. He had the same sexy, long-lashed hazel eyes that could scorch her with a look. Why had she ever tossed him away?

'Oh, I get it.' Burke rocked back on his heels, arms crossed as he surveyed her. 'This little act is one of your looney tunes impulses. Now that you're here, you don't know what to say? Is this just a knee-jerk reaction to my remarriage? Same old Ally!' he jeered. 'You haven't changed a bit.'

His harsh words froze the uncurling desire. Stung, Ally cried out, 'That's not true.'

She bit her tongue to keep from telling him that there was nothing about her that remotely resembled the insecure eighteen-year-old girl he had married six years ago. She had changed, and the process had been painful.

Ally took a deep breath. Instead, she said, with as much dignity as she could muster, as if she were a reasonable adult and he a temperamental child, 'Maybe we should go somewhere to discuss this.'

Burke's voice dropped low. 'You didn't want to talk six years ago,' he murmured silkily. 'As far as I can see there's nothing to discuss now.' His eyes glittered with emotion. 'So take a seat or leave.'

He smirked, as if he knew how much she would hate what he said next. 'I'm getting married, and you can't do a thing about it.'

'Oh, you insufferable lout!' His words incensed her. 'After all the trouble I went through just to get here. It's not my fault I arrived too late to stop the wedding before it started.'

'Would you get out of here so we can get on with this? Now!' Tiffany interjected.

'Go sit down, Ally. You can watch even though you weren't invited,' Burke said.

'You can't get married!' Ally cried, exasperated.

'I said sit down,' he commanded sternly.

Ally's facade of calm serenity evaporated. 'I will not. You can't order me around like an errant child. I have something to say to you, Burke Winslow, and you will listen.'

The murmur from the guests rose in volume to a muted rumble interspersed with laughter. Ally blushed at the realization that the three of them were providing a dog and pony show for everyone.

'Very well, stand there.' He turned his back to Ally and said to the minister, 'Go ahead, Reverend.'

'Uh, Burke,' the minister said with a

gentle smile. 'I can't do that until I hear what the young lady has to say. I'm sure she wouldn't have interrupted such a special occasion unless it was important.'

Tiffany jumped into the conversation. 'Look, Reverend, I'm sure this is just a case of sour grapes. She's probably some cast-off girlfriend.' She checked her watch. 'Anyway, it's getting late. I need to get this over with so I can pack. I've got a meeting in L.A. early in the morning.'

A fresh ripple of laughter greeted her statement. Ally stared at the blonde. She was upset about missing a meeting in L.A.? Was the woman completely blind to the man she was marrying?

Ally looked at Burke. He didn't seem agitated in the least by his bride's remarks. What was going on here?

'Please, Reverend, I'm certain we can sort this out afterwards. Right, Burke?' Tiffany asked.

Burke nodded and muttered. 'Yeah. Sure.' He'd go through with this if it was the last thing he did. He'd show Ally.

'But you can't,' Ally protested.

'Ally, go away.' He kept his back to her. He'd show her how it felt to be rejected. Ignored. Revenge was a bitter brew he was eager to sample. 'You're not welcome here.'

A fresh buzz of conversation greeted his words. The wedding guests were having a field day. By tomorrow, the news of this would be all over Brookwood, he suspected.

Surprisingly, his grandfather had not said a word. Burke turned slightly and glanced over at Frederick Winslow. He was surprised to see the evident amusement on the older man's face. But then Granddad had tried to talk him out of marrying Tiffany.

'Burke, you have to listen to me,' Ally cried.

'I don't have to do anything with you.' He turned this time to face her. His lips curled in an unpleasant smile.

His deliberate rudeness turned up

the heat on Ally's temper a notch. She should just let him go through with his dumb wedding. Then she'd laugh when he found out. But a pain centered around her heart at the thought of his marrying someone else — especially the vision of blond loveliness standing next to him at the altar.

'What is this all about?' Tiffany asked, throwing up her hands as she whirled around.

'Ally, I am getting married, so just go back to Dallas where you've been hiding for the last six years.'

'I'm afraid I can't let you do that,' Ally said. She was surprised that he had known where she lived.

'Just how are you going to stop me?'

His smirk was really getting to her. She jerked her head to the exit door. Just because he was being a horse's ass didn't mean she had to act like one too. 'By telling you something. In private, Burke.'

'I don't think we have anything to say to each other.'

'Stop being so thick-headed and listen for just a minute,' Ally demanded, losing the battle to hang onto her temper.

'Can we please make some progress here?' Tiffany demanded. 'Burke, go talk to her and get back here so we can finish this.'

'Don't call me thick-headed,' Burke said, ignoring Tiffany. 'I'd have thought that you would have grown up a little, but no. You're still the same headstrong girl you were when I first met you. You think you can just waltz in here and wrap me around your little finger again. Well, those days are over, baby.'

'Don't call me baby,' Ally said between gritted teeth.

'Don't tell me what I can and can't do. I'll call you anything I want. Just like I'll get married if I want to.'

'For heaven's sake, you can't get married, you dolt!' Ally blazed.

'And just why not?' Burke fired back.

'Because you're still married to me!'

4

'What?' Tiffany screeched.

Involuntarily, Ally took a step backward, but she needn't have worried. Tiffany's ire was directed solely at Burke.

'Why you — you!' the would-be bride sputtered. Then she smacked Burke in the face with the lilies she held. For a little woman, she packed quite a wallop, Ally thought with grudging admiration.

Yellow pollen rained on his black tuxedo coat and fragments of orange petals fell to the floor. Without another word, Tiffany whirled and stomped down the steps leading from the altar.

'Wait a minute. I can explain!' Burke protested involuntarily, certain that he hadn't a clue as to what was going on. The only thing he knew was that the business deal with Sakamoto Limited was evaporating before his very eyes.

But the overwhelming sense of relief he felt didn't allow him to feel too badly about that fact. The only thing he regretted was the embarrassment for Tiffany caused by this spectacle.

'Wait, Tiff! Tiffany! Come back!' he called out, wanting to apologize yet knowing it was useless. Once Tiff got her back up, it took time for her to settle down.

She didn't look back. 'I'll talk to you when I get back from the coast,' she yelled, punctuating the sentence with a slap of the disintegrating bridal bouquet against her side. To the assembled guests, she waved her hands as if shooing away a flock of curious pigeons. 'Everybody just — just go home!'

A ripple of laughter followed her irate words. Some of the guests rose, but most stayed seated. Obviously they thought the show wasn't over yet, Burke suspected. And in the small town of Brookwood, this had to be the best entertainment around — actually, the only entertainment on a Friday night since high school football was a few months away.

The guests no longer bothered keeping their voices down as they discussed the almost-wedding that would live on almost forever in the memory of the small town. Burke didn't dare risk a glance at his brother and his friends. He knew Rod, Dave, and Craig would never forget this — and they'd make damn sure he didn't either.

Burke sighed. No use throwing caution — and pride — to the wind by chasing after his runaway bride. Tiff wouldn't listen to him until her injured pride recovered. In the past, he'd witnessed her ire at what she considered an insult. He'd often accused her of being related to both the Hatfields and the McCoys because of her talent for carrying a grudge. He shuddered, knowing he was in for it now. It just proved the old cliché: be careful what you wish for.

'Burke?' The minister broke into his thoughts. 'Would you like me to address your guests?'

Burke rubbed his face with both hands, wishing he could wipe away the ill-fated wedding as easily. 'Thanks, Reverend, but I'll take care of it.'

He looked first at his brother Rod and his friends Dave and Craig. Inwardly, he groaned. They were going to have a field day with this. Resigned, he turned to the congregation and was greeted by wide grins and snickers. His side of the church seemed to be taking this in stride. In fact, they seemed to be having a heck of a good time.

Unfortunately, the bride's side of the church was conspicuously empty. Tiffany's family and friends had already departed. He winced. This situation might be more delicate than he'd thought. Tiffany's father and brothers were all bankers in Houston. In fact, they were his bankers. And they weren't noted for their sense of humor.

'Sorry, folks, what can I say?' Burke

shrugged. 'Thanks for coming. If you're hungry, go on over to Ballard's by the Bay. There's no point in wasting all that seafood. And the band should be great. I may even join you later.' He forced a grin, though he felt no amusement at the way the evening had turned out.

With determined steps, he descended the steps from the altar and stopped in front of Ally. In a soft, chilling voice, he spoke, 'To you, I have a lot to say.' He reached out and grabbed her arm. 'I think we'll have that talk now.'

Ally felt her knees turn to rubber at his touch. Oh, golly! She had made a huge error in judgment. Just his hand on her arm made her want to fling herself into his arms. She resisted the urge to do such an insane thing. Instead, she tried to shake his hand loose.

'Let go of me,' she grumbled. Though his grip didn't hurt, it allowed no escape either.

'I wouldn't think of doing such a thing. I know how much you love to vanish when my back is turned!'

Ally swallowed hard. Now she was in for it. She should have slipped out with Tiffany's entourage.

With dragging feet, and feeling as if she were a five year old who was being sentenced to the naughty chair, she allowed Burke to lead her from the church. A loud buzz of conversation followed them up the aisle.

The walk from the altar to the double doors at the back of the sanctuary seemed interminable. Ally lifted her head proudly as if she were accustomed to appearing at social events looking as if she had swum a raging river to get there. She couldn't help the telltale spots of color that bloomed a deeper red in her mud-streaked cheeks.

After she and Burke walked through the big doors at the back, she shook her arm free of his grip.

'That's enough. I'm perfectly capable of walking without your assistance,' she grumbled.

'I just want to make sure you don't

disappear the way you did six years ago.'

Ally had no defense against the truth so she attacked, 'Oh, chill out!'

'Me? Chill?' Burke's voice rose several decibels. 'You've got nerve! You bust in here looking like — like — .' He waved his hands up and down in front of her, seemingly at a loss for words. 'Like that!' he finally exclaimed. 'And break up my wedding. And I'm supposed to chill?'

He shook his head side to side. 'What did you do? Crawl in the rain all the way from Dallas?'

'No, I flew, but I stopped off for some quick mud wrestling,' she quipped, refusing to allow him to see how his words hurt her. So much for her foolish notion that she could impress him with how sophisticated and mature she was.

'What does my appearance have to do with anything anyway?' she sputtered, pulling the hardened strands of hair from her right cheek. She winced.

He looked her over again from head

to toe. 'If you were mud wrestling, it looks as if the mud won.' Then the corners of his mouth tilted.

Ally was furious. 'For your information, Mr. Burke Winslow, I — I — '

His laughter interrupted her. 'Don't you dare laugh at me,' Ally stormed.

'I can't help it. If you could see how you look. I can't begin to imagine how you ended up looking like a drowned rat.'

'A . . . drowned . . . rat?' she asked between clenched teeth. Score a big fat zero for her effort to make him desire her! 'Why, I did it purposely so I'd have something in common with the dirty rat I came to see,' she spat out.

'Uh, uh, uh, Ally. Sticks and stones,' he taunted.

Ally seized the ragged edges of her composure. 'Look, let's forget my appearance. It has nothing to do with this anyway.'

'It has a lot to do with it. It shows how irresponsible and impulsive you still are. You barge in here and break up my wedding on some jealous whim. I'd say I have a right to be upset.'

'Well, maybe I have a right to be upset too!' Ally countered, seething anew. 'And I have a news flash for you, you pompous, arrogant ass. I did not break up your wedding on a jealous whim.'

He cocked an eyebrow at her. 'Are you sure about that? The way I see it, you just can't get over me.'

His words incensed Ally. 'You're crazy if you think I've been pining away for you for the last six years. Why, I've hardly thought of you in all that time because of all the other men in my life,' she lied. A thought struck her. 'How did you know I lived in Dallas anyway?'

'What do you mean?' Burke looked discomfited.

'In the church, you accused me of hiding in Dallas.'

He shrugged. 'Somebody must have mentioned it to me.'

'For the record, I wasn't hiding in Dallas, and I wasn't carrying a torch for you either.' Why couldn't he see that she had become all the things he'd wanted in a woman? She was intelligent, sophisticated, mature, and successful, or so her friends assured her each time they badgered her into allowing them to fix her up with the current 'catch of the day.'

Ally rubbed her arm where his hand had touched her. She swore she could feel the impression of his palm on her skin — it tingled in a way that speeded up her pulse. That had never happened with any of the men she'd dated.

'So tell me, why did you ruin my wedding if it wasn't because of unrequited love?'

'It's certainly not because I like making a fool of myself.' She closed her eyes, determined to put an end to this fruitless bickering. 'This bickering isn't doing any good.' She gestured toward the double doors. 'Those doors are going to open any minute now, and we'll be surrounded by all those curious friends and relatives of yours. I don't know about you, but I'm tired of being the star attraction of this evening's entertainment.'

'Yeah.' Burke looked around. 'You're right. Come on. We won't be disturbed in the church parlor.' He bowed slightly and gestured with his right hand. 'After you.'

Ally directed a withering glare at him. He'd better not burst into laughter again. She whirled and lifted her head regally. 'I remember the way to the parlor.'

During the short walk from the sanctuary to the big room that served as a kitchen and parlor, Ally tried hard to restore her equilibrium. Now was her chance to show Burke how different she was. She'd do that — even if it killed her.

Actually, she was amazed that Burke had accepted her reasonable suggestion. The Burke she'd known years ago would have protested and continued arguing.

Moments later, Burke pushed open

the parlor door. Ally entered the dark room and stopped, unable to see anything. Burke reached out and touched her shoulder. She shivered at his touch.

'Stay here and let me get the lights.' He walked away, leaving her to wonder at the reaction of her nerve endings to a simple touch from him.

She moistened her lips. How would she react if he touched her with more than casual interest? Ally was glad he had not noticed her reaction. She'd have to watch herself. Just being around him called up patterned behaviors. That must be what her problem was, she reasoned.

Fluorescent lights flickered then flooded the room. 'Come on,' Burke said as he walked to the restaurant-equipped kitchen at the end of the room.

Now somewhat more composed and wanting to put an end to what had been a less than brilliant plan, Ally walked to the seating arrangement at the opposite end of the room.

The large room that served as a gathering place for church members had changed little since she'd last been here. An upright piano still occupied one corner and a red-brick fireplace took up the other.

Two long olive green couches separated by a rectangular oak coffee table were arranged perpendicular to the fireplace. A pair of large, overstuffed, rust red club chairs faced the fireplace.

Ally realized suddenly how tired she was. 'I think I'll just curl up in one of these chairs and try to pretend the last few hours didn't happen,' she said.

Forgetting the day's ordeal and the embarrassment of the evening would take some doing, though.

'No offense, but I think you should go to the rest room around the corner and, shall we say, freshen up?' Burke said, his eyes glinting with amusement as they swept her from her straggling hair to her muddy shoes.

Looking down at herself, Ally had to

agree. She was too filthy to even perch on the edge of the chair's seat.

'Good idea. Would you excuse me?'

'Of course.' Burke bowed from the waist. 'How could I refuse such a formal request?'

Ally refused to spar with him anymore. 'Jerk,' she muttered beneath her breath as she smiled at him.

In the ladies' room, Ally caught sight of herself in the mirror and nearly shrieked. She looked much worse than she had imagined. Sophisticated and desirable? Ha! No wonder he wasn't impressed!

Her sleek, shiny hair had been replaced by a dull, mud-colored mess hanging from the side of her head. Gravity seemed a certain winner over the single hair-pin that precariously held it. Her best dress was a disaster.

With lots of water and all the paper towels in the dispenser, she tried to improve her appearance. When she turned her attention to her hair, she realized that her comb was in her purse

— in the rental car.

'That blasted car!' She had completely forgotten that crumpled blue problem. She still had to straighten all that out with the guest who owned the Jag.

Ally said a quick prayer that the rental car would start so she could get back to the airport before her flight left tonight. That is, assuming Burke didn't do her bodily harm after she told her little tale.

'That will have to do,' she told her reflection. Why couldn't she look like the woman she'd worked so hard to become? She might not be the model-thin girl she'd been when Burke had married her, but she looked good.

More importantly, Ally had made peace with herself. She no longer saw the chubby, unhappy teen who'd dieted and exercised herself to thinness just to get into a bikini the summer after her high school graduation. Though once thin, she'd never looked at her reflection without seeing a fat girl looking back. She was thankful she had changed.

Poor Burke! When she'd met him that summer day, he'd had no idea that her first bikini hid more than the vital parts of her anatomy. It also hid the insecurity of the transformed chubby teen. That insecurity had given birth to the worst kind of jealousy. It had eaten at her like acid whenever Burke had been anywhere near another woman. That was really what had destroyed her marriage.

At least she'd gained something from losing the only man she'd ever loved. She had discovered herself. She was a few pounds heavier now, but she was comfortable with that fact and with herself.

Ally frowned, remembering the vision of beauty that Tiffany had presented at the altar. She stuck her tongue out at her reflection. Feeling drab next to Tiffany was as ridiculous as her supposed motivation in coming here, she decided, leaving the restroom.

Burke had made himself at home in the kitchen. He was intent on his task and didn't notice her. She soaked up every detail of his appearance from his thick, sandy hair to the soles of his polished shoes.

His face had matured attractively. Faint lines fanned out from his intoxicating eyes, and added character to his face which now revealed a tough strength.

Just as his face had matured, so had his body. Gone was the lean adolescent build. He was well-muscled and filled his clothes in a way that made her wonder what he looked like without them.

Burke wasn't the twenty-two year old she'd fallen in love with. He had become a man — a very desirable man. Tuxedos were unfair weapons in the war between the sexes. No man should have such an advantage over a woman. To her discomfort, he looked drop dead sexy in the classic black suit.

The scent of his musky aftershave

teased her. She watched silently as he measured water for the coffee-maker. She found her gaze fixed on his hands, large and tanned, as they completed the simple task.

A shiver coursed down her spine. She remembered a time when his hands had touched her and made her insane with longing. She shook her head and roused herself from her reverie.

'Want me to do that?' she offered. When they'd been married, Burke had been in charge of the kitchen. She couldn't even boil water. 'Your coffee is memorable, but not because it was good.'

'You know how to make coffee?'

His words surprised a laugh from her. 'Is that so shocking?' The laughter eased some of the tension from her.

He grinned. 'When we were married, you couldn't even boil water.' His gaze lingered on her freshly-scrubbed face. He'd nearly forgotten that captivating little dimple at the right corner of her mouth. Even under the ceiling fluorescent lights, her skin glowed.

'Well, that was six years ago,' she said, grinning.

It took Burke a moment to realize what looked different about her. She was tanned. Her arms looked toned, appealingly muscled. She wasn't model-thin any longer. He liked that.

He couldn't pull his eyes away. The sleeveless dress revealed a body that would make a man take a second look, and a third. He frowned. He didn't like that idea at all.

'Right, six years,' he murmured, barely listening to what she was saying as his eyes searched out the differences in her appearance. Her body was riper. She'd looked great when they'd been married, but there was something about her now that stirred an interest he'd prefer not to feel.

Ally was rounder. Fuller. His gaze moved across her breasts. Riper. His hands itched to trace the curves of her body.

'You were completely inept in the kitchen,' he said, somewhat unnerved by her nearness.

'I'm a lot more ept now.' Ally chuckled.

'I would hope so,' Burke said, turning his back so she wouldn't see the desire in his eyes.

Ally was glad that Burke had turned away. His gaze made her want crazy, unattainable things, but he belonged to another woman now. That thought filled her with despair. There was no use torturing herself.

'Look, I need to get back to the airport as soon as possible — and there's a little problem with my transportation.' She waved her hands as if to dismiss her words. 'But that's my problem, not yours. In any event, my return flight to Dallas leaves in a couple of hours. So why don't we get to it?'

Get to it? The words hammered at him. Burke didn't trust himself to reply. He'd love to get to it with her — but not the conversation she had in mind. He clicked the coffeemaker on and proceeded to open the cabinet door. On the pretext of selecting coffee mugs, he took time to corral his wayward thoughts.

After a moment, Ally said, 'Burke?' She frowned. His ignoring her reminded her too much of the past. This was more like the Burke that she knew. Too often he'd ignored her when she'd tried to talk to him. Irritated, she reacted like the Ally he knew. She smarted off.

'If we hurry and finish, maybe you can catch your cute little bride before she hops the plane for the coast.' Ally cringed as soon as the words were out.

The idea of Tiffany being described that way struck Burke as hilarious. 'Tiffany? Cute?'

Ally bristled. 'What's so funny?'

'I don't think I've ever heard Tiffany described quite that way before.'

'Well, she's just the cutest little thing I've ever seen.' Ally couldn't seem to help herself. 'Just the way you like your women, right?' As soon as the words left her mouth, Ally wished she could call them back. How could she convince him she'd changed with spiteful comments like that?

'I guess you should know. After all, you're an expert on the kind of women I like. Right?' Her jealous words called up all the hurt from the past. 'I don't play that game any more, Ally,' Burke said quietly.

Ally looked away. 'I know how that sounded.' She took a deep breath and apologized. 'I'm sorry. Let's just forget I said that.' Her eyes entreated him. 'It was just a bad joke,' she said lamely.

'Okay,' he agreed, surprised by her apology. 'Let's just forget it,' he said stiffly, unconvinced by her about-face. He didn't have to indulge her jealousy any more. Her possessiveness had destroyed their marriage. Gone were the days when he tried to make Ally believe in him and in his love.

'After all,' he said aloud what he was thinking, 'I'm not married to you any more.' He frowned. 'Or am I?'

'Don't frown, Burke. This awkward situation can be easily remedied. Then you'll be free to marry Tiffany.' Sadness filled Ally. She'd been wrong to come here. She should have called. Why hadn't she?

Ally's soft comment again surprised Burke. He had to fight the urge to tell her that his wedding was just a business arrangement. What was it about the woman that made him want to explain? Made him want her to believe him? Hadn't he learned anything? He bet if he pushed the right buttons, Ally's control would shatter in a second.

Maybe she'd throw a tantrum the way she had when they were married. Then he'd get over this . . . this desire to pull her into his arms.

'Tiffany is everything a man could want.' Once, those would have been fighting words to Ally who seemed to view every female between the age of sixteen and sixty as a threat.

Ally clamped down on the green monster which suddenly reared its ugly head. She just bet the blond bimbo was exactly what men wanted. But she wasn't going to let him see that his words incited her to jealousy.

'Then you must feel very lucky,' she said calmly, and walked away. Glancing back at him, she caught him staring at her as if thunderstruck. Good, she thought. Let him see that she was confident and unaffected by petty emotions.

'I'm sure if I got to know Tiffany that I'd like her very much,' she added for good measure.

Burke felt an odd emotion at her words. He couldn't figure out why he suddenly felt so depressed. Shaking his head in confusion, he filled their coffee mugs, adding milk and sugar to Ally's.

Suddenly, it dawned on him why her words upset him. Ally couldn't still care for *him* if she was so calm and placid about Tiffany. And, perversely, that bothered him. Shaken, he stood holding the steaming mugs of coffee and stared at her as she strolled around the room. He didn't want her to be unaffected, damn it.

He tried to tell himself it was for the best. No one could live on the emotional roller coaster he and Ally had ridden for the nine months of their brief marriage. Why, just look at the torrent of emotion she had unleashed simply by coming here tonight. They'd sniped at each other and flung insults just like in the old days. Old habits were hard to break, he guessed. He took a deep breath and began walking toward her.

'Well, I guess it really is over,' he said lightly. But he didn't really believe it. 'I had some crazy thought that, despite what you said, you really came here to reconcile with me.' He knew that if he had more time with her she'd revert to old habits.

'Reconcile?' Ally laughed. 'Why, what a thought, Burke.' She was proud of her performance. 'How silly.'

'Yes, I guess it was my overactive imagination,' he joked, feeling more uncertain by the minute. Could she really no longer care? At her continued laughter, he said testily, 'It wasn't that funny!'

Ally smiled. 'The first time you and Tiffany get to Dallas, we'll have to have dinner together.' That would be when Texas folks wore snowsuits in July, she thought, keeping her fake smile in place.

'Oh, yeah. Sure. That will be fun,' Burke said as he handed her the coffee mug. An awkward silence fell between them. Was it really, finally, over between them?

Burke seated himself on one of the couches. Ally turned away and set the mug down on the coffee table. She blinked the mistiness from her eyes and sat on the other couch opposite him. She was being silly, but she felt as if she'd lost him all over again. She swallowed hard, refusing to give in to maudlin sentiment. Their relationship had ended long ago. Apparently, she just hadn't accepted that fact.

'Yes,' she said bravely. 'Dinner with you and your w — , with you and

Tiffany will be lovely.' As if interested, Ally pretended to study the design on the coffee cup. Why did she feel so desolate? She'd made a good life for herself without Burke. But if she could change what had happened six years ago . . . She risked a glance at him. He made her want to throw the past — and caution — out the window. No other man had ever had this affect on her.

'So tell me why you broke up my wedding,' Burke asked.

'Oh, yeah.' Ally took a deep breath. Being near Burke, she felt like a poor little moth contemplating the flame. 'You're sure you're ready to hear this?'

'Quit stalling. At the moment, I'm calm and relaxed, but I've waited about as long as I can. So start talking. What's this all about?'

He might be calm now, but it was just the calm before the storm. 'I think I'll need this to make it through my story.' She sipped her coffee, then grimaced.

'What's the matter? Didn't I put in

enough milk and sugar to disguise the taste of coffee?'

'Actually, I drink it black now.' She felt oddly pleased that he'd remembered how she'd drunk her coffee.

'Oh.' He looked sheepish. 'I'll get you another cup.' He reached for the mug. Their fingers touched and suddenly all Ally could hear was the sound of their breathing. She forgot what they were talking about.

'What?' she asked breathlessly. She fought the temptation to close her eyes and lean toward him.

'Huh?' Burke asked. His eyes looked deep into hers.

Ally's breath caught in her throat. She moved her index finger a millimeter. It slid against his for a brief moment.

Burke's hand jerked. Coffee sloshed over the rim of his mug and onto his fingers. 'Ouch!'

The spell was broken. 'Are you all right?' Ally asked, pulling her mug from his hand.

'Sure.' He pulled his handkerchief from inside his coat pocket and wiped his fingers.

'The coffee is fine this way,' she said hurriedly. 'I don't mind it at all.'

'Okay. Go on with your story,' he said, settling back. Burke's pulse raced like a quarter horse pounding the track. His hand felt shaky. He made a fist and squeezed it. He nodded at Ally and gave her a tentative smile.

When she smiled back at him, Burke stared at the tiny dimple that peeked out from the corner of her mouth. He remembered kissing that dimple. And suddenly, the only thing he wanted was to kiss it again. What was between them couldn't be over. It just couldn't be if he still felt this need, this hunger for her.

Whatever passion had drawn them together still smoldered, he decided. At least it did in him.

Time seemed to stop for an instant. When it started again, his heart pounded at double speed to catch up.

Ally stirred up impulses that would get him into all kinds of trouble.

He was six feet two inches of trouble, Ally reminded herself. And he didn't belong to her any more. She needed to get this situation taken care of and then her life — and his — could get back to normal. She'd go home to Dallas and continue her peaceful life. Her peaceful, dull, boring life, a little voice inside her amended. That was what she wanted.

Wasn't it?

5

'You remember when we decided to get divorced?' Ally asked.

Burke's brows shot up. 'Decided to get a divorce? The way I remember it, there was no decision. You decided on your own to get one. I had no say in the matter.'

'Well, you precipitated the matter, as I recall.'

'Yeah,' he said, disgust shading his voice. 'So do I. You were in a jealous rage when I came home late after a study session — '

'A study session with that woman you spent more time with than with me!' Ally said, trying to keep her voice calm.

'And you launched into an all out attack, listing my so-called flings since we'd been married.' Burke scowled. 'I don't know how you think I'd have had the energy to carry on with that many women when I was working full time, not to mention trying to finish my master's degree. Baby-sitting you and trying to keep you happy was a full-time job in itself.'

'Baby-sitting me? Is that how you saw our marriage? Why, you . . . you . . . ' Ally couldn't think of anything foul enough to call him. Guilt rode her hard. He was more right than she wanted to acknowledge, but the truth hurt. She lashed out at him. 'You insensitive, arrogant — '

Dismayed that she'd lost control, she clamped her lips shut, refusing to give in to her roiling emotions. She wouldn't give him the pleasure of thinking she was still that immature. With immense effort, she controlled her anger, but hurt colored her words.

'Look,' she bit the words off as if they tasted bitter, 'I didn't come here to get into that. All I'm trying to tell you is what happened. I was upset. You told me if I really thought you were running around, then I should go ahead and divorce you. So I did. I just forgot to sign the darn papers and get them filed.'

'You forgot?' he asked, his disbelief evident. 'How could you forget a thing like that?'

'It was easy. I was upset.' She blew her breath out and stared at him as if daring him to challenge her.

'Upset? You don't know upset.' He slammed his mug down on the coffee table so hard, black liquid sloshed over onto the varnished oak.

'Well, if you're so smart, why didn't you realize they hadn't been filed? Didn't you think it strange when you never received copies?'

Burke retrieved his mug and gulped his coffee. It burned all the way down. He didn't look at Ally nor reply. He remembered how he'd thought maybe she had come to her senses. After a while, he'd somehow forgotten to pursue the matter.

'Well, don't you have an answer?' she prodded.

'I was upset too,' he muttered, not looking at her and not willing to give her the satisfaction of knowing that he'd thought she would come back to him.

Ally was speechless. Was that hurt she heard in his voice? She cleared her throat. 'Yes, well, that's understandable.'

'So how did you find out that we weren't really divorced?'

'I had a call from my grandmother. You remember Granny Edith?'

'The one who lives in Galveston, right?' He grinned. 'Yeah, I remember her. I always thought she and my Granddad would have hit it off.'

'Oh, no.' Ally shook her head vigorously. 'I don't think they'd have anything in common.'

'Sure they would.' He rolled his eyes. 'But that's beside the point. We don't need to get into an argument over it. Go on with your story.'

'Granny called me at the office today. She said she'd been cleaning out the attic where I have some things stored.

In one of the boxes, she found the divorce papers. She looked them over and realized they'd never been signed.'

Ally shrugged. 'I don't know how, but she knew that you were getting married today and thought she should tell me.'

'Wow. I can't believe it. Still married after six years of living single.'

Ally bet his single life had been more exciting than hers. Oh, she'd dated, but not seriously. Of course, she'd been busy with college and establishing a career.

Preston Kesey was the only man she dated regularly, but instead of a lover, Preston had become her best friend. Neither of them wanted more than friendship, but, she decided, Burke didn't need to know that.

'This news will certainly put a crimp in my social life,' she said, 'but I shudder to think what would have happened if I hadn't stopped your wedding.' Ally much preferred him to think she had to beat the men off with a stick.

'Yeah,' he said. 'A conviction for bigamy isn't something I want to list on my resume. I suppose I should thank you for arriving when you did. I just wish it hadn't been quite so dramatic.'

'You and me both. Making a spectacle of myself isn't my idea of fun. Too bad Tiffany didn't stick around to hear the explanation.'

'Well, she probably wouldn't have had time anyway. She still had to pack.' His voice trailed off.

'Yes, so she said.' Ally couldn't help herself. 'I don't mean to be nosy, but she seemed rather, uh, oddly concerned with business.'

'Oh, that.' Burke's ego rallied to the occasion. He was horrified that Ally would probably think he couldn't get a woman. He resented the fact that no woman had ever come close to inciting the emotion in him that Ally had tapped. This was his chance to show her that she didn't still have a hold on him. Because she didn't!

'Well, Tiff and I are business partners

first and foremost.' Let Ally infer whatever she pleased from that fatuous statement, he decided.

Ally dropped her eyes. 'Oh. How convenient.'

'Tiffany is a woman in a million,' he elaborated, choosing his words carefully. 'We've been business partners for years. We share the same priorities in business and life.'

'How nice,' Ally murmured. *I am not jealous of that itty bitty witch. I am not jealous*, she mentally chanted.

'We've been together long enough for our relationship to withstand the test of time,' Burke said expansively. He wasn't exactly lying, he rationalized.

'How wonderful,' she murmured.

'Our company needs an influx of capital to expand. That's created a lot of problems. That's one reason Tiffany reacted so oddly. She's stressed out. She's really a wonderful person. I'm sure you would see that if you got to know her.'

'Oh, I'm sure,' Ally said. When pigs

skydive, she didn't say.

Burke looked at her closely. Was she mocking him? 'Anyway, we hit a brick wall in our expansion plans. Tonight was just an example of, uh, frayed nerves.'

That's all he would say, Burke decided. Let her go back to Dallas and then he'd worry about getting financing from Sakamoto Limited — without having to take a wife to do it.

'So you'll go on with your wedding as soon as this, uh, business problem is taken care of?'

'Oh, sure,' he lied. 'When you've been partners as long as Tiffany and I have, you take things like this in stride.'

Partners, huh? Ally gritted her teeth. Why didn't he just say lovers? 'I see,' she managed to reply. 'It sounds as if you had a great arrangement — the best of all worlds with none of the legal entanglements. Why spoil a good thing by getting married?'

Burke shrugged. 'To make a long story short, in order to close this deal, I needed a wife. Japanese investors are extremely conservative. The individual who owns Sakamoto Limited is even more straight-laced than is usual.

'According to my sources, he views our company as too risky because Tiffany and I jointly own the company and neither of us are married. So we decided to eliminate the problem by formalizing our arrangement.'

'Eliminate the problem? Formalize the arrangement?' Ally's voice trailed off as if she hadn't heard correctly or didn't believe what she'd heard. She shook her head. 'That sounds like you're writing a five-year plan, not falling in love. You and Tiffany were getting married because you needed a wife? To close a business deal?'

'And he still needs one.' Burke and Ally turned at his grandfather's voice.

Frederick Winslow stood in the doorway. 'That coffee smells good. Think I'll join you in a cup.' He grinned at them.

'Granddad, I didn't hear you come

in.' Burke wasn't surprised to see his grandfather. Frederick Winslow seemed to have a knack for being in the center of action in everything. He suspected the man missed his glory days of bossing oil drilling crews.

'What I mean to say is that the chick has flown the coop. Tiffany's dad came back in and told me that they'd be bobsledding down the highest hill in Hades before he'd let his daughter go through this farce again.'

Burke shrugged. 'Can't say I blame him. Guess Tiffany and I are back to square one.'

He didn't sound very upset about the situation, Ally thought. Maybe he wasn't as committed to Tiffany as he wanted her to think.

'So what are you going to do, son? You still need a wife. Looks like your partner has decided it's not going to be part of her job description.'

Burke shrugged. 'I'll think of something.'

'I guess I've made a mess of things,'

Ally said uncertainly.

'Did Burke tell you everything?' Frederick Winslow asked. Before she could answer, he said, 'It's a good thing I decided to pop over here. I can shed some light on this situation.'

Burke cringed. With Ally's attention on his grandfather, Burke shook his head and pressed his index finger to his lips in an effort to warn the man not to say anything else.

His grandfather had never been enthusiastic about this particular wedding and would no doubt spill the beans to Ally that Tiffany and he had never even had a date. He'd make sure Ally knew every detail about Burke's extremely limited social life.

Unfortunately, Frederick Winslow either didn't understand or he chose to ignore the warning. Knowing how quick-witted his grandfather was, Burke figured the tall, white-haired man who'd raised him and Rod had decided, for whatever reasons, to ignore Burke's warning because he plunged ahead.

'Did you tell Ally why you and Tiffany came up with this wild scheme?'

'A little,' Burke muttered. He was going to be humiliated. 'I was just about to, uh, clear things up when you walked in.'

'Well, don't let me stop you. I'll just be quiet as a mouse.'

That would be the day, Burke thought. 'Granddad, I'll take care of this. You can go on home. I'll drop by later and fill you in,' Burke said.

'Oh, that's too much bother for you. I'll just hang out here for a while.' Frederick raised his long arms over his head and stretched. 'I got tired of listening to all the gossip over in the church. You'd think those people didn't know there was a perfectly good baseball game on tonight. They could be home watching the Astros beat the heck out of the Rangers, but they'd rather flap their jaws about you and Ally.'

Burke and Ally groaned in unison.

'Let me get my coffee. Go ahead, Burke. Don't mind me.' Frederick served himself, then came over and sat next to Ally on the couch.

Burke didn't miss the glimmer of amusement in his grandfather's eyes. Looked like the old man was actually enjoying this little comedy.

'I was telling Ally about Sakamoto Limited. You see, Ally, my company has developed software that will revolutionize the computer industry.'

'What's the name of your company?' She asked.

Burke grinned. 'Byte Me. Spelled b-y-t-e.'

'That's cute,' Ally said, laughing. 'So what does Byte Me do?'

'We design and manufacture computer software, mostly for novice users. Our new product makes it possible for any computer user to customize their desktop more easily than ever before. Someone will be able to go in and compose a list of the software they want in their machine. Our software will then go through a search and destroy, organizing the software requested and then automatically deleting everything else that is not wanted, including duplicate files, icons on the desktop, everything that was bundled and sold with the computer.'

'Wow. That's remarkable.' Ally felt an undeniable sense of pride for his achievements. 'I've wanted to get rid of that excess stuff, but I discovered that if you delete a program you don't want, then another program you might want could be affected and not work properly.'

'Exactly. Our software will analyze every file of every program that you want and then configure the entire system to work properly. Just think of the market for a product like this. We've worked for four years to develop it.'

'When Burke and Tiffany first went into business, they bought the old Havenpark Social Club building,' Frederick said.

'It didn't cost much to remodel it for

producing our first products, mostly games, but we need to expand and upgrade the facility before production can be started on this new project,' Burke said.

'So that's where Sakamoto comes in,' she summed up.

'Right. We need a substantial capital investment to get underway. Of course, we'll recover the start-up expenses in a relatively short period of time.'

'I see why this is so important to you,' she said.

'Even by Japanese standards, Sakamoto is terribly old-fashioned. He thinks that a man and woman who are business partners, and not married to each other — '

'Are engaging in some kind of hanky panky on the side,' Frederick finished. 'Isn't that a hoot? And he's not some old codger like me, either, Ally.' He snorted. 'But don't let me interfere with your story. Go on, son.'

'As I was saying — ' Burke tried again.

'Heck, that man acts as if women and men can't work together without their hormones getting the better of them and wrecking the company,' Frederick interjected. 'He ought to know by looking at your financial statements that you and Tiffany don't have hormones!'

Ally choked back a laugh, but she didn't say anything.

Burke winced. 'Thanks, Granddad. You want to tell the rest of this story?'

'Shoot, no, son, you're doing a great job.' The older man leaned back and sipped his coffee. 'Go on.'

'Sakamoto also thinks that an unmarried man is an unstable man. According to his philosophy, married men have more at stake and work harder.'

'So to make a long story short,' Frederick interrupted again, 'if Tiffany and Burke want the money, they have to get hitched to somebody. So they decided getting hitched to each other was the perfect answer.'

Burke rolled his eyes. 'Well, I'm glad I finally had the chance to tell this story,' he muttered. He looked at his grandfather. Frederick's blue eyes twinkled with mischief.

Uh-oh. Burke knew that look. He'd seen it every time Frederick had tricked him and Rod into doing something they didn't want to do — such as getting them to work at the local hamburger joint rather than hitchhiking to Alaska to work on a fishing boat which the brothers had decided they must do one summer. Well, it wasn't going to work this time. Whatever *it* might be.

'That's a very, uh, interesting story,' Ally said. Was Burke involved with Tiffany or wasn't he? She wondered. She felt a glimmer of hope that this marriage of his was nothing more than a convenience.

'Well, I'm sorry I upset your plans.'

'Yeah, I can hear the regret in your voice,' Burke muttered.

After a sip of coffee, Frederick said, 'You clean up real nice, Ally. But then you always were a pretty girl.'

Ally smiled. 'Thank you, Mr. Winslow.'

'Now, now. Don't call me Mr. Winslow. You called me Granddad before, and I assume somehow or other that you're still married to my grandson so you're still entitled to call me that. And I won't take no for an answer.'

'All right, Granddad. So is there more to this story? Any deep, dark secret about the righteous Mr. Sakamoto?'

'Sakamoto is coming here next week. I guess Burke will lose the deal, even though their company would be a perfect investment for Sakamoto.' Frederick frowned. 'Maybe it's just as well. This deal has Burke and Tiffany acting like a couple of clowns.'

'Thanks, for explaining everything so succinctly,' Burke said dryly.

'Aw, shucks, son. I just feel real strongly about making a travesty of the sacrament of marriage, even if you seem convinced that good business partners make good marriage partners.'

He sighed loudly. 'Though I guess if you marry someone you like, there's always the chance that you could grow to love them. What do you think, Ally?'

Ally studied the coffee in her cup as if it held the answer to that difficult question. When she'd been married to Burke, all he seemed to care about was getting ahead — despite her own immature fears that he was seeing other women.

Apparently, Burke's career was still the most important thing in his life. In Tiffany, he'd found a woman who fit into his plans perfectly.

'Yes, I think love can grow between two people,' she said softly. She pictured Burke with the beautiful Tiffany, day after day. And night after night. It might start out as a business arrangement, but given the intimacy of the situation, he was bound to succumb to Tiffany's charms. He wasn't the kind of man to choose a celibate life. With sinking spirits, she realized that she'd only managed to delay the inevitable.

'Tell me what brought you to Houston, Ally,' Frederick said. 'Guess there must have been something wrong with that divorce you got.'

'Dear old cousin Will who handled my divorce didn't have enough sense to follow up. Guess that's why he only practiced law for a year,' she said, lightly.

'Well, I'll be a ring-tailed possum.'

'Granddad, don't you think that's overdoing it a little?' Burke asked dryly.

'But I'm just amazed as all get out,' Frederick said. 'I mean, you need a wife, Burke. As it turns out, you've already got one!'

6

'Oh, no. Don't even think what you're thinking,' Ally warned. Impersonating his wife wasn't what she had bargained for. It ran a distant second to what she wanted, she realized.

'Why not? This would be the perfect answer to my problem,' Burke said. He cocked his head to the side and studied her as if appraising her for the role.

'I am not the answer to your problem.'

He hadn't changed, Ally realized. His career still ranked number one in his life. And he had Tiffany for number two. He didn't want her back. He just wanted his stupid business deal to succeed.

'I didn't come here to be your wife, Burke. I came to get our divorce back on track. We need to do whatever is necessary to make it official.'

'We can do that too as soon as the deal goes through, if that's what you want.'

Hurt by his easy agreement to the divorce, Ally said, 'Good. That's exactly what I want. I don't want to be married to you any more than you want to be married to me.' He need never know that part of her had wished that he'd take one look at her and fall for her all over again. What a hopeless romantic she was.

Burke said, 'You're certainly in a hurry to be legally free. Why is that? Got someone waiting in the wings?'

Ally met his eyes across the room and knew she'd lied to herself when she'd decided to return here. She hadn't just wanted him to see the woman she had become. She'd wanted him to fall in love with her again.

Oh, Ally, you fool!

'Well, do you have a boyfriend waiting for you?'

The devil made her do it. That is the only excuse she could come up with for her reply. 'Why, yes, I do. And he's just the most wonderful man in the world.'

Burke's brows snapped together. 'I see. No wonder you wanted to get this divorce processed.' He paused a moment, then said coolly, 'For now though, you're still my wife.'

Ally slammed her coffee mug onto the table. 'Quit saying that. I am not your wife.'

'That's not what you said in the church less than an hour ago,' Burke reminded her. So she had another man, huh? It hadn't taken her long to replace him. After all, it had only been six years. Why was she in such a hurry?

'I did not come here to break up your wedding because I wanted to be your wife again. I'd have to be insane to want that, wouldn't I?'

'Thanks a lot,' he said. His mind worked furiously. This could be his chance. Whoa! He applied the mental brakes. His chance for what? To show Ally that he didn't need her. Right? Or was it something else?

He pushed the thought away. This was a chance for revenge. What else could it possibly be? She'd broken his heart, and now she'd come back to stomp on it, with tales of her new boyfriend, for good measure. Well, he'd show her that she didn't have any hold on him any more.

'I mean,' Ally added hastily, 'it's not as if you've been sitting around waiting for me to come back to you, now is it?'

'You're right. I'd have to be crazy to have expected — or wanted — that.'

'Good. Fine. Then we're agreed.' Ally forced herself to reach for her coffee as if the matter were settled. She sternly commanded herself to get this over with and leave before she made a worse fool of herself.

'But you are still his wife,' Frederick said with a chuckle. 'It sure would solve a lot of immediate problems.'

'Stop saying that, Granddad. I'm not his wife.'

'Methinks thou doth protest too much,' Burke said, eyes glinting.

'Well, you can think whatever you doth please.' Her heart pounded in a confusion of emotions.

Her vehement protests put his back up. 'Granddad's right,' he needled.

'No, he's not. We're married in name only.'

'Well, that's okay. It would be a business arrangement just like Burke and Tiffany were going to have,' Frederick put in. 'A marriage of convenience.'

'I don't think so, Granddad,' Ally said, trying not to shout. She was willing to bet that the business Burke and Tiffany were engaged in was monkey business as much as computer business. Even if they weren't, did the elderly man really think that Burke would have kept his hands off Tiffany for long? Maybe Frederick Winslow had forgotten what it was like to be in intimate quarters with a member of the opposite sex, but she hadn't.

How could she possibly have a marriage in name only with Burke, the one man — the only man — who excited every nerve ending in her body?

Burke studied the panicked expression on Ally's face. What was she so upset about? Was the idea of being his wife so abhorrent? *His wife*. The two words had an unsettling effect on him. He told himself it was just because he was excited over finding a solution to his immediate problem. Teaching Ally a lesson would be an extra bonus, though.

'Actually, Burke,' Frederick insisted, 'Ally's coming here is the answer to all your problems.'

When Ally squawked in protest, Frederick said, 'Just hear me out. What you've proposed is brilliant.'

'I didn't propose anything!' Ally protested.

'Ally, you can't run away and leave Burke in the lurch. You're the one who put him on the spot. If you had signed the divorce papers the way you should have, then he wouldn't be in this predicament. Or if you had let him know before now. But you showed up and sent Tiffany flying. The way I see it, you're responsible for this mess.'

'No, Granddad!' she said.

Frederick stood, then swayed as if disoriented. He pressed his hand over his forehead. 'Oh, my!'

'What's wrong?' Burke leaped to his grandfather's side and grabbed the elderly gentleman's right arm. Ally rushed to his other side.

'Here, sit down,' she urged. 'Let me get you some water.' She dashed to the kitchen and was back in an instant.

'Now, now, don't fuss over me,' Frederick groused, sipping the glass of water she pressed on him. 'I guess I'm just so stressed out by this whole situation.'

Ally felt terrible. 'I'm so sorry,' she said contritely.

Lines of worry creased Burke's forehead. 'Do I need to call a doctor?'

'No, no. I'll be fine. Just a little dizzy spell. Guess this has all been too much excitement for me.'

Ally and Burke's eyes met over Frederick's head. Her eyes questioned. His accused. Burke shook his head and shrugged his shoulders, at a loss to explain his grandfather's attack of vertigo. Frederick hadn't complained of any health problems.

As far as he knew, his grandfather was in perfect health. Worried, he faced the fact, for the first time, that Frederick Winslow wasn't a young man any more.

'I've just been so upset over this Sakamoto deal that my blood pressure has gotten out of control,' Frederick said.

'I didn't know you had a blood pressure problem,' Burke said, feeling guilty. He'd been so busy that he had neglected his grandfather the last few weeks. Had that been when Frederick started suffering from high blood pressure?

'Well, it's not something I brag about.'

Burke studied Frederick closely but

his grandfather didn't look any different than he ever did. In fact, he looked to be the very picture of good health. Puzzled, he wondered about this sudden blood pressure problem.

'Just relax,' Ally urged. 'We won't talk of this any more.'

'No, we need to talk about it,' Frederick insisted. 'Burke has to play host next week. Ally, your plan is his only chance. You two are still married. It's the perfect answer. Even if Burke wanted to get divorced and remarried, he couldn't accomplish it in enough time. And that's assuming Tiffany still wants to go through with the marriage.'

'This is emotional blackmail,' Ally wailed.

'Oh, dear,' Frederick gasped and closed his eyes.

'There, there,' Ally said, hurriedly. 'I didn't mean to — '

Burke shushed her. 'That's enough for now. We'll talk later,' he muttered, as much puzzled as concerned.

Contrite, she realized he was right.

But she had to return to Dallas. She wouldn't be able to handle a steady diet of Burke Winslow.

'Ally, you owe this to Burke,' Frederick insisted. 'If it hadn't been for you, he'd be married by now.'

'It's not my fault,' she protested feebly. But in her heart, she felt guilty.

'You're the one who stopped the wedding, aren't you?' Frederick asked.

'Yes, but . . . but it wouldn't have been legal,' she stammered.

'Sakamoto wouldn't have known that,' Frederick said.

'Yes, but — '

'And Burke has worked too hard to lose everything now.'

'Granddad, the deal isn't that important,' Burke said with a shrug.

'Not important? Then why were you and Tiffany going to marry just to make it work?'

Burke frowned, uncomfortable at the question. The deal was important but wouldn't shut him down if it didn't go through. Maybe his priorities were out of kilter. Perhaps work had become too important. It had been the only thing that kept him going after Ally was gone.

'Think of all the embarrassment you caused Tiffany and her family,' Frederick said, 'not to mention the ridicule Burke will receive.'

'Yes, but — ' Ally's voice was softer than before. She felt that she was fighting a battle she couldn't possibly win.

'To sum it up,' Frederick said, pressing her hand, 'You've sabotaged Burke's future.'

Ally felt miserable. 'That's not what I intended. I didn't know the consequences of this.'

'I believe you, child. But this is your chance to make it right. Play the role of Burke's wife for the next month. Then when the papers are signed, you and Burke can file for divorce. That's what you want, isn't it?'

'Of course it is,' they both said in unison.

Ally wavered. They were asking far

more than she was willing to part with. How could she be next to Burke, day in and day out — not to mention the nights, the voice of temptation whispered — and not fall completely in love with him again? This wasn't what she'd expected! But she didn't want to upset Frederick any more than he already was.

Burke watched Ally as she considered Frederick's scheme. He really should be honest with her and tell her that the fate of his company didn't hang in the balance. But something held him silent. Maybe Ally did owe him something for leaving him the way she had six years ago. He looked her up and down, certain that she was unaware of his perusal. Maybe he just wanted to find out if she still went up in flames when he kissed her.

Kissed her! What was he thinking? Get a grip, he commanded himself. There would be no kissing. This was just going to be a marriage of convenience. Just the way it would have been if Tiffany had gone through with the ceremony.

He reminded himself that Ally's long-ago jealousy had destroyed their marriage. She'd broken his heart.

His resolve hardened. 'Decide now. Tell me one way or the other,' he told her brusquely.

'Give me a minute! I'm thinking.' Ally worried her lower lip with her teeth as she considered all the ramifications of this little deal. She knew it was a mistake. Somehow, she would have to find a way to play Burke's wife yet keep her emotions in check. She looked up at him and sighed. Otherwise, she'd never get out of this intact.

'This is a dumb plan,' she protested, 'but I guess I have no choice.'

'It may be dumb, but I don't have a choice now. I've got thirty employees, and their families, to think about. It's not just my future. It's theirs too,' he defended. Somehow, he didn't feel a pang of guilt at coercing her with half-truths.

Ally twisted her hands. 'I didn't think of it that way.'

'You never did — think, that is — in the past, so why should you be any different today?' he muttered.

'That's not fair. I am not the silly, starry-eyed girl I was six years ago.'

Burke looked her up and down. 'Except for some obvious physical differences — ' His left brow arched. 'I can't see that you're any different.'

'That's insulting. It doesn't seem as if you have changed much either.'

'Oh, but I have. I'm not the trusting soul I once was. You cured me of that,' he said.

'I could say the same if we are going to trade insults. One thing is certain. You're still the same autocratic, arrogant chauvinist that I was married to. That's an excellent reason for us to make this divorce official. So if I have to play your wife to get this divorce, then fine!'

'Children, children. You're giving me a headache. Stop arguing. You'll have those nosy people from the church poking their heads in here at any moment. Maybe I should leave you two alone to thrash this out. As they say, three's a crowd.'

'No, don't go,' Ally pleaded, not wanting to be alone with Burke. 'You need to rest.'

'I feel much better. But you still need to work this out with Burke.'

Frederick ambled over to the door and paused. 'Now, you two work out the details. I know you both are sensible, mature adults. Put the past behind you. Forget that passion you once had. Don't even think about all that lust and sex.'

★ ★ ★

As soon as Frederick left the parlor, he pulled a tiny cellular phone from his coat pocket and placed a call.

'Hi, darlin',' he said. 'It went like clockwork, even better than we planned. I've stirred the pot, and they should just about be coming to a boil real soon.

'I'll be glad when these kids get

straightened out.' His voice dropped to a husky whisper. 'Then maybe we can have a wedding of our own.'

A grin broke over his face. 'I should be at your place in about an hour. Will you wait up for me?'

He was still smiling broadly as he punched the button to end the conversation.

* * *

After his grandfather left, Burke was silent. Should he come clean with Ally and tell her that his business wouldn't fail if this deal didn't go through? He remained silent. Some perverse imp inside him didn't want her to leave just yet.

'It's agreed then. You'll be my wife.'

The words struck a chord deep in Ally's heart, and despite herself, she smiled.

'For a month,' he added.

Ally's silly smile faded as if it were a chalk sidewalk drawing washed away by a bucket of water.

'As long as I get the divorce for real.' She needed to sever the tie between them once and for all.

'That's what we both want. Right?' he asked.

'Indeed.' Ally's pride demanded that she not allow Burke to think she had such a lackluster life that she could walk away from it so easily. 'I want the right to continue seeing my — ' she choked on the word *lover*. She couldn't lie quite so blatantly. 'My friend,' she concluded. 'I don't want this arrangement to interfere with my relationship with Preston,' she bargained.

'Preston?'

'Preston Kesey, the man I mentioned? He and I are,' she took a deep breath and plunged in, 'such special friends.'

'Yeah?' Burke's mouth twisted in derision. 'Special friends, huh?' He felt a wave of anger sweep through him. 'What does he do for a living?'

'What has that got to do with anything?'

'I just want to make sure he can support you properly.'

'You're living in the Dark Ages, Burke. Women don't need a man to support them any more.'

'Aha! So he's unemployed!' He felt a savage satisfaction.

'He is not. He's an artist of some renown. His work is in collections from the East Coast to the West. Actually, he's quite a celebrity.' Ally crossed her fingers. Poor Preston, he really was talented, but his work just hadn't caught on yet.

Burke made a rude sound. 'A celebrity, huh.'

'Now what's wrong? When you thought he was a bum, you were delighted. Now that you realize he isn't, you're a grouch.'

'Are you and this Pearson living together?' he asked, ignoring her complaint.

'Preston,' Ally corrected. 'No, we are both terribly independent,' she said brightly. 'We keep separate residences but it's rather pointless since we spend most of our time together. He's expecting me tonight. That's why I wanted to leave for Dallas as soon as possible.'

'Can't stand a night away from him, huh?' Burke looked more sour with each passing minute.

Ally stared at Burke in surprise. Why, he sounded jealous! He couldn't be envious of a man he'd never met. Especially not over her.

'That's right. It's difficult to be separated,' she said, watching his expression carefully. She was amazed to see the muscles in his jaw clench and unclench as if he were chewing on something unpleasant.

Impossible as it seemed, he was jealous. Ally recognized the symptoms. She'd been the victim of that negative emotion all the months of her marriage to Burke. Oddly, the knowledge that he was jealous exhilarated her. She should feel sorry for him, she chastened herself, because she knew from experience how devastating jealousy could be.

'How old is he?'

'My, so many questions.' Ally couldn't have been more surprised by this unexpected turn of events. 'I think Preston must be a year or two younger than I.'

'A younger man!' Burke pounced on the tidbit as if he'd been awarded a prize. 'That's disgusting.'

'Why?' she asked, eyes wide and innocent.

'Why? Well, everyone knows why that's disgusting,' he muttered.

'I guess I must not be everyone because I don't see anything wrong with it.'

'You wouldn't. Surely you don't dally with every Tom, Dick, and Pearsall that comes along.'

'What are you implying? I don't dally with — ' She broke off. So he was jealous, was he? How many times had she been consumed with that negative emotion because of him? He hadn't cut her any slack. Wasn't turnabout supposed to be fair play?

She looked right into his eyes, lowered her voice to a soft purr and said, 'I don't dally. I'm completely serious when it comes to my men.' To her delight, the color in his face rose to an alarming shade of red as if he might explode any minute.

Satisfied with this little experiment, Ally toyed with the idea of having Burke walk the full mile in her shoes. Let him learn how jealousy could make a person absolutely miserable. Maybe he'd learn some compassion from the experience.

His hazel eyes held hers. She'd never be able to spend a month around him. Not even to teach him a lesson. Not without jumping his bones.

'I think a month may be too long. Let's say a week,' she said.

'Impossible! It's got to be a month,' Burke replied quickly.

She shook her head. 'Nope. That won't do. I might be able to manage two weeks.' She pursed her lips thoughtfully. 'I suppose I could get Preston to look after my apartment,' she said, just to gauge his response.

His lips tightened. 'Fine,' he snapped. 'Do it. I'm sure Percy can manage without you for two weeks.'

'Preston,' Ally corrected with a soft sigh. She hoped Preston never found out how she'd misrepresented their relationship.

'When does this marriage of convenience begin?' she said. 'I'll need to go home and pack.'

'Oh, no. I'm not letting you out of my sight. I'll buy you whatever you need.'

'Don't be ridiculous. I'm not going to refuse to come back.' She couldn't think of anything that would keep her away from delivering this lesson.

'I believe you. Let's just say a new wardrobe is my treat — a bonus to seal the deal.'

Ally started to argue but was interrupted by Frederick. He strode in, looking hale and hearty as if his dizzy spell hadn't happened.

'Burke!' Frederick called. 'You're not going to believe what happened to your Jag.'

7

An hour later, a small crowd, mostly male, had gathered in the dark to watch a tow truck haul away Ally's rental car. Headlights of the remaining cars in the driveway illuminated the scene.

Every man there had gone over and run his hand over the scratched fender of the Jaguar as if to soothe the beast, Ally thought, finding a little humor in the scene. Men were so funny where cars were concerned.

'Ally, I got to hand it to you. This has been one of the most entertaining Fridays since I got home from college,' Burke's brother Rod said, grinning like a monkey.

'Yeah, that's me. Miss Entertainment.' Her lips twisted in a weak smile.

'Do you do birthdays, or just weddings?' Craig Bishop asked.

'Call my agent. We'll talk,' Ally

muttered, looking over to where Burke stood with Dave Hernandez. Both men stared dolefully at the Jaguar.

The tow truck driver finally had the rental car hitched up. Ally signed the appropriate papers and turned away. At least the rain had stopped.

'So what do you do for an encore?' Rod asked.

'I haven't decided,' Ally said. 'Probably just something minor like put my foot in my mouth.' She wanted to apologize again to Burke, but he and Dave Hernandez were still conducting some kind of wake by the fender of the Jaguar.

Then Burke looked over at Ally as if just remembering her presence. 'Come on, Ally.' He pressed a button on his alarm pad. The Jaguar chirped.

His tone of voice put her back up immediately. She didn't move. Instead, she and Burke conducted a staring contest. He blinked first.

'Okay,' he said, pursing his lips and nodding. He walked around and opened the passenger door. 'Now!'

'Don't bark at me,' Ally said, standing her ground. Someone, Rod she thought, laughed, but then quickly suppressed it.

'I'm not barking. I'm making a perfectly reasonable request for you to get over here and into the car.'

'With you?'

'No, with Brad Pitt. Of course, with me.'

'Don't be sarcastic. Maybe I don't want to go with you. I'll get a ride with your brother.'

Rod held up both hands and backed away. 'Oh, no. I may be just a dumb college kid, but I'm smart enough not to get in the middle of this.'

Ally turned to Craig. Before she could even speak, Craig said, 'Sorry, Dave and I rode over with Rod.'

'Now will you get in the car?' Burke demanded.

'No. You're still mad about the scratch.'

'The scratch? Is that what you're

calling the two foot square area where the paint is abraded?'

'Abraded? You make the car sound like a person who's been mugged.' Ally stared at the muscle in Burke's jaw. It popped in and out as if he were chewing nails. Maybe she'd been a tad testy.

'I really am sorry about your car,' Ally said for perhaps the tenth time.

'Let's just drop it,' Burke suggested.

'It's not as if she did it on purpose,' Rod said.

'Right,' Ally chimed in. 'And besides, it's just a scratch. I don't know what the big deal is.'

'I'll tell you what the big deal is. That car represents a heck of a lot more than transportation.'

'Oh, yes. A man and his car. It's your status in life, your corporate image.' She rolled her eyes.

'No, it's the first thing I bought with my own money. It's long hours unbroken by anything except hard work. It's the reward I gave myself for putting my nose to the grindstone after you walked out on me.'

'Wow, all that, huh?' Ally said lightly, not wanting to give voice to the sympathy his words elicited.

'Let me give you some advice, Ally. Since you dropped in, you've busted up my wedding, insulted me, chased away my business partner, and wrecked my car. I'd say it hasn't been a good evening. So, one, don't tell me what to do. And two, get in the car. Now!'

Her sympathy dried up. 'You might intimidate your business associates with that roar, but it doesn't cut it with me.' His scowl looked ferocious enough to scare the pants off anyone, she thought, feeling as if she were poking a sharp stick in a lion's face.

Unrestrained laughter greeted her words.

Burke threw his hands into the air. 'I give up. You are the most infuriating —!'

'Don't even think it, Burke,' his friend Dave counseled him. 'The prison term wouldn't be worth it.'

Even Ally had to struggle not to smile at that.

'Granddad, would you help me out here?' Burke implored.

Frederick laughed and took Ally's arm. 'Come on, child. Burke gets kind of cranky when he's tired.'

Burke rolled his eyes but didn't say a word. He slid onto the luxurious leather seat and waited.

Frederick held the car door open for Ally. When she was seated, he said, 'Burke will get you settled in for the night. You look kind of bushed too.'

'I am,' she admitted, suppressing a yawn.

'Just remember,' he said softly so only she could hear, 'his bark is a lot worse than his bite.'

'I don't know, Granddad,' Ally whispered back. 'He looks as if he'd like to take a bite out of my hide right now.'

Frederick laughed. 'Looks are often deceiving, child. He might want to bite you, but not in the way you think.' He winked at her. Then he slammed the car door.

Burke started the car and rocketed away from the curb as if afraid she might put up further resistance. As soon as he'd put a couple of blocks between them and the church, he slowed to a normal speed.

Ally was intensely aware of his presence in the close confines of the car. Frederick's advice had surprised her. Thoughtfully, she studied Burke. Her husband. The word made her feel warm all over. She'd never have guessed this day would have ended with them driving away together.

After a minute, she said, 'I didn't know Brookwood had a motel now.' She gazed out the darkened window as Burke drove along the oak-lined main street.

'It doesn't.'

'Then where are we going?' She turned to look at him.

'Where do you think? To my house.'

Ally's heart thundered. 'Oh, no. I

don't think so. Just turn this car around and take me back to Houston. You can drop me off at the first motel you come to.'

Burke's hands tightened on the wheel. 'No way.'

'I'm not staying with you tonight.'

She could see his smirk in the darkness.

'Don't worry, Ally. Your dubious virtue will be safe with me.'

'Do you go out of your way to insult me?'

'No, it just comes naturally,' he said.

'What do you mean by that crack about my virtue?'

'Hey, you're the one who bragged about your conquests.'

'I did not!'

'You did. You said you didn't dally. That you were serious about your men. Men is plural. What other conclusion should I have drawn?'

Ally growled in frustration. 'You are impossible.'

'Besides, your antics this evening

have completely worn me out. I'm too tired to drive into Houston. You have to get used to my house sooner or later, so it might as well be sooner. It's going to be your home now, you know.'

'Only for two weeks. And the clock doesn't start until tomorrow as far as I'm concerned.'

'This is ridiculous,' Burke snorted. 'What's the difference between tonight or in the morning?'

'Plenty. So just drive me to Houston.'

'You certainly have become a demanding woman. When we were married, you never asked for anything — other than my undying attention twenty-four hours a day,' he finished sarcastically.

'That's because my self-esteem is a heck of a lot healthier now than it was then.'

'What does that mean?'

Ally clamped her mouth shut. She wasn't about to bare her soul to him. 'Believe me, I don't want your attention — not even for twenty-four seconds,' she said.

'Good, because you're not getting it. And you're not getting a ride to Houston either.'

Her temper flared. 'I may have gotten more demanding, but you've become impossible.'

'Get used to it. And get used to the idea of staying in my house. It's part of the package. Don't worry. I have no designs on your virtue.' He smirked.

She'd like to slap that smirk off his face, she thought. She chewed on her lower lip. 'I agreed to this under duress. I don't think I gave it enough thought. You and your grandfather rushed me into this deal before I could think it through. We didn't even set any ground rules.'

'Ground rules?' He laughed, but he didn't sound amused.

'I may have been railroaded into doing this, but I insist that we set some rules. I want it clearly understood what is allowed and what isn't.' That should keep him at arm's length, she hoped.

'This is not some kind of dating game, Ally.'

'I beg to differ.'

'You're my wife.'

'I'm posing as your wife,' she interjected.

'That means you have to be comfortable around me and my home. So you must live at my house.'

'Act as if I live at your house.'

'You'll be my hostess, and fulfill all the duties of a wife.'

'Ha! You mean pretend to fulfill all the wifely duties.'

'Yeah, whatever. Pose, pretend.' Burke sighed. It was obvious his patience had worn thin. 'I give up. There — does that satisfy you?'

'I guess so. But let's get back to this sleeping at your house tonight.'

'Ally!' he groaned.

She held her hands up. 'Just listen. I didn't come prepared to stay in Houston. I don't even have a toothbrush, much less a nightgown.'

'Then I'll stop and get you one.

There's a twenty-four-hour drug store in Brookwood.'

'Okay. I'll need some face cleanser, facial scrub pads, toner, night cream, eye cream, moisturizer, deodorant, dental floss, toothpaste, a vent brush, shampoo — ' Ally, determined not to make this easy on him, went on and on, listing everything she could think of.

Burke said in amazement, 'You need all that for one night?'

'More or less,' Ally said, glad that she was proving to be an annoyance. He'd regret making her stay in his house.

'When we were married, you never used all that face stuff.'

'Well, I'm older now. I have to be more careful about my looks.'

'Doesn't Piercey object when you crawl into bed with that greasy goo all over your face?' he asked testily.

'Well, I don't use it when *Preston* is around,' she said nastily.

Burke fell silent. He didn't like the mental picture playing in his head. He hated the thought of her and another man.

'Okay, let's get what you need and go home,' he said, swinging into the drugstore's parking lot.

An hour later and nearly two hundred dollars poorer, he hustled Ally into the car and slammed the door. He was amazed that cleaners and moisturizers had such high price tags. He was equally amazed that a woman had to have all that stuff just to go to bed at night and look halfway presentable the next morning.

Driving away, he grumbled, 'Well, are you satisfied now?'

'I still need a nightgown and something to wear in the morning.'

'You're out of luck. Brookwood doesn't boast an all-night department store. You'll have to wait until tomorrow to go clothes shopping. You can use tonight to draw up your list. I'm sure it'll be extensive,' he said dryly.

'Well, what am I going to sleep in?'

Burke had a suggestion, but he didn't

think she'd take kindly to it. But the thought of her wearing nothing but a smile put a smile on his face.

'What are you thinking about?' Ally demanded.

'Nothing.' He cleared his throat. 'I can find something for you for tonight, but you'll just have to wear what you've got to go shopping in the morning.'

'If you'd just let me fly home, I could pack and be back in a couple of days.'

'Somehow, I don't trust you to do that so let's not discuss it again.'

'What do you plan to do, spend every minute with me to ensure that I don't skip town?' Ally grumbled.

'If necessary.' He glanced at her from the corner of his eye. Actually, that wouldn't be much of a hardship.

Ally sighed. 'All kidding aside, I really do need to go back to Dallas fairly soon. I've got an office, a job, and clients that I am responsible to.'

He frowned. 'I didn't think of that. Will your boss fire you if you take off?'

Ally couldn't resist the opportunity

he offered her. 'Actually, I'm the boss.'

'What do you mean?'

'It's my company. I own a small accounting firm.'

'A number cruncher, huh? I must say I'm surprised.'

'I've worked hard to get ahead. I'm good at what I do. I love my work. And my clients love me.'

'Well, if you're the boss, then it shouldn't be a problem,' he said, as if that closed the subject.

Ally realized she shouldn't have been so eager to impress him with her accomplishments. 'Right,' she admitted reluctantly. 'I can have my assistant handle things — unless an emergency arises.'

He looked at her appraisingly. 'Good. I never suspected you had a head for business. You always hated the fact that I was so driven, but I suspect you're a little bit driven too. It's not every woman who owns her own business two years out of college.'

His assessment warmed her. She

unbent a little. 'I guess I could use a little time off. I worked so hard to get through college and then to prove myself that I've never had a real vacation.'

The idea of her working that hard made him uncomfortable. 'I would have given you the money to go to college,' he said impulsively.

'It was better for me to do it myself. I didn't even take help from my parents.'

They rode in silence for a while. Ally noticed they had entered a residential area of subtly lit mansions set on beautifully landscaped lawns.

'Do your parents know you came down here?' Burke asked suddenly.

Ally shook her head vigorously. 'No, and if I'm lucky, they won't find out. They still haven't gotten over our sudden marriage — '

'And equally sudden divorce?' he finished.

She nodded. 'I never could figure out why they didn't put up a bigger fight when you showed up a month after we met with an engagement ring in your pocket.'

'Engagement ring?' He laughed. 'I don't know if that pinpoint diamond could properly be called an engagement ring. Did you toss that pitiful excuse for a ring into the Trinity River on your way back to Dallas when you left me?'

Ally didn't say anything. She still had that ring and the matching gold wedding band. It still brought a tear to her eye each time she came across them in her jewelry box.

'Is this your neighborhood?' she asked, changing the subject.

Burke turned left into a driveway that curved toward a huge contemporary house made of cedar, stone, and huge expanses of glass. It gave an overall impression of sharp angles thrusting against the night sky. He pressed a button on the dash as he drove to the rear of the house. A double-size garage door opened, and he pulled into the garage and parked next to a huge black pickup truck.

Ally was awestruck. She'd done very well in her career, but Burke had obviously done better with his software company. 'This is yours?'

'Be it ever so humble.'

'Looks as if all your hard work paid off in a big way.' She felt disquieted by the signs of wealth everywhere. When she and Burke had married, they'd been on an equal economic footing. Both his and her families were solidly middle-class.

At the back door, he punched in a security code on a keypad then made a sweeping bow to her. '*Mi casa es su casa.*'

'Yeah,' she sighed. 'I guess your house is my house — but only for a couple of weeks.'

8

Three days later, Ally decided that if she couldn't get to a supermarket to stock up on some munchies, she would probably die of starvation before the two weeks were up.

She hurried down the wide hallway that led to the master bedroom. The hidden spotlights overhead weren't on and she was thankful that she didn't have to look at Burke's collection of art that lined both walls. She hated the abstracts. They were cold and lifeless, just like everything else in the house.

When she'd commented that she didn't know he liked modern art, he'd said, 'I think my taste in art probably runs more to dogs playing poker. This is investment stuff. It's appreciated a hundred and fifty per cent since I bought it.'

'At least it's good for something,' she

muttered as she passed the huge canvases. Personally, if she were going to invest in art, she'd make sure it was something she liked. Even if it was only pictures of tough-looking canines playing draw poker.

Ally took a deep breath before she knocked on his bedroom door. When he didn't answer, she called, 'Burke? Are you awake?' She'd made a point to get up before seven so she could catch him before he had breakfast. When there was no answer, she knocked harder, hoping Deirdre Henry, his housekeeper, didn't hear her.

Deirdre the Drill Sergeant should be preparing Burke's breakfast, though, so it should be safe. After a minute, Ally eased the door open and peeked in.

She could hear him before she saw him. He snored softly. 'Burke, are you awake?' Dumb question, she thought. He had overslept. She looked down at him. The covers were tangled about his waist. His muscled chest was covered with a fine sprinkle of hair that was sandy-colored, just as Ally remembered. One hairy leg lay exposed.

Ally's tongue darted out to moisten her suddenly dry lips. In the dim morning light, he looked like every woman's dream. Too late, she realized that his snoring had ceased. The blanket moved as if it had a life of its own.

'See something you like?' Burke asked, his voice husky with sleep and something else that she didn't even want to think about.

'Not particularly,' Ally lied. 'Sorry I had to wake you, but there's something we have to discuss.' She made her voice brusque and businesslike.

He patted the side of the bed. 'Sit down, and tell me what it is.'

Ally's heart pounded. 'Oh, no thanks. I'm fine standing. Thanks anyway,' she babbled.

'Not afraid, are you?'

'Why on earth would I be afraid?'

He shrugged. The blanket moved. Ally's eyes examined the extra inch of skin that the shifted blanket exposed. Oh, my goodness, she thought, imagining sliding her hand under the blanket and stroking that beautiful body of his.

Abruptly she turned away. 'I can catch you later. It's not really that important.' She headed for the door.

He uttered one word in a deceptively quiet voice. 'Chicken.'

That stopped her cold. She turned. 'What did you say?'

'You heard me. You don't trust yourself around me.' He folded his arms beneath his head and stared into her eyes.

Ally could not stop her eyes from glancing at the covers to see how much more of him had been exposed. Oh, no, she groaned inwardly. She closed her eyes and took a deep breath. 'I don't know what you're talking about,' she said, but her voice came out weak and breathless.

Her sexy whisper teased Burke. He'd been dreaming about her and had opened his eyes to see her standing over him. It had taken every ounce of his will not to reach for her. He wanted to pull her down on top of him.

'We're both mature and unattached, Ally,' he said, his voice soft and cajoling. He reached out to her. Slowly, as if mesmerized, she walked toward him. She placed her hand in his. When he pulled gently, she yielded and stepped closer.

'Mr. Winslow, your breakfast is ready!' a stern voice barked from the intercom on the wall.

Ally jumped as if someone had poked her with a sharp pin. 'I'll talk to you over breakfast,' she said, and ran out of the room.

'Little coward,' Burke said to the empty room.

*　*　*

Ally studied her flaming cheeks in her bathroom mirror. 'You are an idiot, Ally Fletcher!' Her voice trembled with emotion. She closed her eyes, but that only intensified the pictures in her head.

'Oh, Burke,' she breathed, remembering the way he looked with the tangled covers, revealing much, concealing more. His eyes drugged her with remembered passion. His husky voice teased her and dared her.

'What am I going to do?' she moaned. He had hardly been home the last few days, but instead of that helping, it merely made her hunger for a glimpse of him.

Last night, she'd stayed awake until she'd heard him come in around two this morning. Where had he been? Who had he been with? The questions tortured her. Damn it, he was driving her crazy whether he was here or gone. She had to get away from here for a while. All the more reason to brave his sly glances and confront him at breakfast. At least Deirdre would be there so she wouldn't have to see him alone.

After a quick pep talk, Ally left the

guest room and headed to the kitchen. She no longer paused in awe in the two-story great room even if it was big enough to hang glide from the second floor balcony.

Now she only saw the beautiful oak paneling. At least the warmth and richness of the wood made up for the stark white the interior designer had used. She would have been scared to death to drink a cup of coffee while sitting on the huge white sofas. She was even fearful of walking too close to the wall of white draperies at the end of the room for fear she'd stain them.

That first night she'd arrived, Burke had looked around the room as if seeing it in her eyes. 'I guess it's kind of cold, isn't it?' he'd asked.

Ally had hedged, 'Well, monochromatic color schemes are all the rage, I understand. It's really very sophisticated.' She'd hated it, but it was better than the kitchen.

'That's what the decorator told me,' he had said, nodding. 'She explained that the different textures of tone on tone provided visual interest.' He'd wrinkled his nose. 'Personally, I thought something in red or yellow would be more interesting, but Tiffany convinced me that the decorator was right.'

'Ah. Tiffany.' Ally's green-eyed monster had peeked out. 'Maybe I could change the throw pillows. Add a few in red or yellow, if you like?'

'Sure. Do whatever you want,' he'd said. Then Ally had looked around with interest. She'd lain in bed, daydreaming about what she'd do if the house were hers.

Hesitantly, Ally stepped into the huge kitchen, and shuddered. Most hospitals didn't have this much stainless steel in their operating rooms. Dark granite countertops gleamed coldly in the fluorescent light. She was certain they'd be suitable for surgery.

A stove big enough for the pickiest chef occupied the center of one wall. Everything was pristinely clean even though the smell of bacon and eggs and fresh-brewed coffee scented the air.

'Good morning, Mrs. Henry,' she said, forcing a note of cheer into her voice.

Ally felt the same way she'd felt when she'd first been introduced to the woman: as insignificant and as pesky as a house fly. She somehow felt that Mrs. Henry would like to swat her away from her stainless steel palace and blizzard-white realm.

She checked to see if the woman had a fly swatter anywhere near before asking, 'May I have a cup of coffee please?'

'Of course,' Deirdre said in a voice that held no emotion whatsoever.

'Make that two,' Burke said.

Ally jumped. 'I didn't hear you come in.'

Burke reached for the two cups of coffee Deirdre had poured. 'Bring breakfast out to the pool, would you please, Deirdre?'

The pool and flagstone patio were the saving grace of the home. Ally could easily have spent every day sitting under the bougainvillea-covered trellis and gazing at the sparkling blue pool that curved around the back of the house.

Ally had finally got the nerve up to open the draperies each day when Deirdre finished vacuuming that part of the house just so she could see the pool from the great room. The view was simply spectacular. She could get used to seeing that tropical scene every morning.

She sank into her favorite chair facing the pool. A miniature waterfall cascaded down from a pile of rocks at the end of the pool and splashed cheerfully into the crystal blue water.

'You like this, don't you?' Burke asked, taking the chair next to hers.

'I can truthfully say that I adore it. It almost makes up for the rest of the house.' As soon as the words were out, Ally covered her mouth with her hand. 'Oops. I didn't mean to insult your home.'

'So you don't like it. Why not?'

'I'm not into the operating room look

in kitchens,' she quipped.

'I told you to change whatever you don't like. I meant that. I want you to be comfortable here.'

'What's the point? I won't be here that long. And the next Mrs. Winslow might not like my taste any more than I like the taste of that decorator you hired. Right?'

Burke felt his good mood slip away. 'Right,' he snapped and turned his attention to the housekeeper.

She pushed a tea cart over to their table and then straightened. Ally thought she looked as if she might execute a military salute.

'Mr. Winslow,' Deirdre said. 'I need to go over the party preparations with you today.'

'I've got a full day scheduled, but I'll call you later.'

Deirdre's lips thinned. 'Very well.' She did a sharp about-face and marched back to the kitchen.

Ally grinned. 'Are you sure she wasn't in the army?'

He grinned. 'She's a retired school-teacher, Ally.'

Ally shuddered. 'Bet those kids were glad to celebrate her retirement.'

Burke offered her a basket of breadstuffs. 'She is a bit grim, but you can't fault her cooking.'

Ally selected a raisin scone and reached for the butter. 'Too true,' she said, biting into the warm bread. She moaned her pleasure.

At the sound, Burke looked up. He'd love to make her moan like that — deep and low in her throat. He shifted uncomfortably on the seat and adjusted his napkin strategically. Ally had the most unsettling effect on him.

Ally caught him looking at her and blushed. She gulped her coffee, thankful that it had cooled enough not to scald her tongue. Suddenly, the intimacy of the breakfast scene struck her. She and Burke were behaving like a married couple.

The click of the garden gate intruded. Ally looked askance at Burke just as

Tiffany strode into view. And the morning had been so nice until now, Ally thought unhappily.

'Hello, Burke,' Tiffany said.

'How did the meetings go?' Burke asked.

Tiffany acknowledged Ally's presence with a stiff nod. Ally nodded back.

Tiffany seated herself next to Burke and began a detailed report of her Los Angeles meetings. Ally studied the woman as she talked. Tiffany wore a white linen suit. The jacket was shaped to her body, and the skirt barely hit below midthigh. The woman obviously thought her legs were an asset. Unfortunately she was right.

Next to the crisp, unwrinkled Tiffany, Ally felt sloppy in her yellow T-shirt, blue jogging shorts, and sneakers. Her only consolation was that if Tiffany walked into the house, she'd be nearly invisible in the white on white. That thought brought a grin to Ally's face. When she heard the word party, her ears perked up.

'What's this about a party?' She asked. 'Mrs. Henry mentioned it too.'

'The party for Sakamoto,' Burke said.

'I don't know anything about this,' Ally replied, a little uneasy. 'When is it to be?'

'Next week when he arrives, of course,' Tiffany said, speaking directly to Ally for the first time. 'It's business.'

'What!' She shook her head in disbelief. 'When had you planned to tell me about it?'

'What's the big deal?' Burke asked. 'I'm telling you now.'

'How many people will be at this party?'

He shrugged. 'About a hundred, I think.'

'A hundred! And you don't know what the big deal is?'

'It's being catered,' Tiffany said, but her comment fell on deaf ears. She shrugged.

'You won't have to do anything,' he said. 'Everything has been planned.'

'We'll use the usual caterers,' Tiffany

interjected. 'They're very — '

'I don't believe this,' Ally interrupted. To Burke, she said, 'How am I supposed to throw a party by next Saturday?'

'I told you, it's being handled. Besides, just think of it as part of the job.'

'I'm not getting paid enough to think of it as part of the job.'

Tiffany's eyes rounded. 'You're paying her for — '

Burke interrupted her, 'Well, how about I double what you're getting?' He and Ally locked eyes and neither backed down.

'Oh, just peachy. What's two times zero?' Ally asked.

'Uh, maybe I should leave?' Tiffany said.

'Look, Ally, it's no big deal. A hundred people might sound like a mob, but, believe me, there's no boisterous behavior or excitement, unfortunately. These things are deadly boring.'

'Then maybe I'll duck it. I hate boring parties,' she said.

'I don't think so. You're the hostess with the mostest. Maybe you'll liven things up.'

'You should have just hired someone to pose as your wife,' she grumbled.

'That wouldn't work. No backing out now. You're my wife, and you'll darn well act like it.'

Tiffany stood. 'When I'm around you two, I feel as if I'm invisible. I'll see you at the office, Burke.' She didn't bother saying goodbye to Ally before she stomped away.

'What got into her?' Ally asked.

Burke shrugged. 'I guess she didn't want breakfast.' He looked at his watch. 'I've got to fly.'

'We haven't finished discussing this.'

'Yes, we have. I think there's a guest list on the writing table in my bedroom. Look it over and we'll talk later.'

He turned to go. 'Oh. I guess you'll need something to wear to the party. I forgot about it when we were shopping

Saturday.' He reached into his pocket and pulled out his wallet. He tossed his platinum card down on the table. 'Use this. My treat. Maybe shopping will use up some of your nervous energy so you'll be too tired to argue tonight.' He grinned. 'And take the Jag. The keys are on the writing table in my bedroom.'

Ally's mouth dropped open in mock surprise. 'You're trusting me with your prized possession? I'm honored.'

'Don't be a wiseass.' His grin took the sting out of his words. 'Just be careful with the Jag.'

9

Ally changed into tan slacks and a matching sleeveless blouse. She ran a brush through her hair and applied some lipstick before she went to Burke's room.

As soon as she stepped through the doorway, she could smell his aftershave. She inhaled deeply and closed her eyes. How intense would the scent be if she pressed her lips to his skin? His presence was so strong in the room, Ally shuddered as if he'd touched her.

She looked longingly at the massive bed that occupied the middle of the immense room. Deirdre had already made the bed and vacuumed in here. Even though the monochromatic-loving decorator had struck here too, Burke's bedroom had more personality to it than the rest of the house.

His presence was stamped on the room by the musky scent of his cologne, by the paper-strewn mahogany writing table, and by the book, a Tom Clancy novel, lying face-down on the bed table.

With him gone, she tested the bed, flinging herself into the middle of the huge ivory quilted spread. Just lying here and dreaming about Burke made her dizzy with longing. She stretched and then luxuriated in the feel of the quilted silk spread, turning her face into the covers to enjoy his scent.

After a few minutes, Ally rose, not wanting to take the chance that the stern housekeeper would find her lounging on the boss's bed. But she couldn't help thoughts of what might have been.

She saw the keys on top of the stack of papers on the writing desk. Then she noticed the paper beneath the keys. Ally plucked the keys off the stack and read the message written in bold, block letters.

Meet me at the office for lunch at noon — if you're not too chicken.

'Oh, you insufferable man!' she exclaimed. She turned on her heel and left his room, forgetting in her irritation to straighten the spread where she'd lain.

★   ★   ★

Burke sat in his office and stared out the window. He'd got himself in a pickle. All he could think about was Ally. He should be concentrating on the typed reports on his desk, but he'd given up on them an hour ago.

Impatiently, he checked his watch. Another hour before noon. Would Ally show?

A tap on his door brought him out of his reverie. 'What's up, Dave?'

'Just thought I'd let you know that I'm bringing Clarissa tonight.'

'Great. Did you tell Meg already?' At Dave's nod, Burke asked, 'How many does that make?'

'I think Meg said she'd made reservations for seventeen, just in case Ally's grandmother feels like driving up from Galveston.'

'Excellent, excellent. I offered to send someone after Mrs. Fletcher, but she would have none of that. Maybe if she comes, Ally won't feel so much like an outsider.'

Burke stared out the window. He didn't notice the kids playing in the park across the road, nor their mothers who watched them. In his mind's eye, he was seeing Ally. At least, he was seeing her the way he wanted her to be tonight when he brought her home from dinner — relaxed and in a good mood from the camaraderie of his friends, the great food, and the frozen margaritas. Burke grinned.

'Uh, Burke?' Dave asked.

'Oh, sorry, Dave.' Burke turned back. 'Anything else?'

Dave chuckled. 'I guess not. Somehow I have a feeling you won't be worth killing until the next two weeks are past. And I'm not referring to Sakamoto.' He lifted a hand to stop Burke's protests. 'It's cool, man. Oh, thought I should tell you. Frederick's on his way up.'

Burke watched his friend and vice president leave. Unfortunately, Dave was right. He couldn't seem to focus the way he normally did. And he couldn't seem to stop fantasizing about Ally. Having her share his home had backfired on him.

What did he want where Ally was concerned? He'd thought he wanted revenge. Instead of plotting vengeance, though, he spent most of his waking hours scheming how to get her in his bed and his sleeping hours dreaming about the same thing.

When his grandfather poked his head in, Burke waved him in. 'You know, Granddad, this is all your fault,' he accused.

'Uh-oh. What have I done now?'

'It's Ally.' Burke ran his hands through his hair. 'She's driving me nuts.'

'Well, what's she doing, Burke?'

'Lots of things.'

'Like what?'

'Well, she walks around there in shorts and a T-shirt. She could at least put something over her legs,' he blustered. 'And then she does her hair so it's half up and half trailing down her back — makes her look as if she'd been rolling around in bed. And she paints her toenails that bold, sexy red so even they look provocative.'

'Yeah,' Frederick said wryly, 'I can see how that would upset a man.'

'And, the way she smells.'

'Stinks, huh?'

'No! If only she did! It's that perfume she wears. I walk in at night and smell her scent as soon as I step into the living room. It makes me — ' He broke off. His face flushed. 'Never mind.'

'Still a sucker for her, huh?' Frederick asked with a broad grin.

'The more I'm around her the more confused I get,' Burke said. 'I should have bundled her off to Dallas when I had the chance.'

'Well, it's not too late. You can get Meg to make a reservation for the next flight.'

'No, I can't do that.'

'Why not? It's a simple problem that can be solved with a phone call to an airline.'

Burke fidgeted. 'It's just not that easy.'

'Why not?'

'It's just not. Okay? Let's change the subject. Have you decided to come to dinner with us tonight?'

'I might drop by. Got to run now. Just wanted to check out the lay of the land, so to speak.'

★ ★ ★

Frederick could hardly wait to get out of Burke's office so he could make his call.

'Darlin', it's going great. Things are progressing just the way I figured they would. Like grandfather, like grandson,

I guess.' He chuckled, then asked, 'So tell me, have you looked over the calendar and selected a date for us yet?'

* * *

When Ally drove up to Burke's building, she saw Frederick sitting in his car. He was talking on his cell phone. At least this was a good sign. Maybe her luck was changing. As soon as she saw him set his phone aside, she ran to him.

'Granddad, you have got to help me.'

'Why, Ally, what are you so upset about?'

'I need you to take me to the airport as soon as possible.'

'What? Why would you want me to do that?' He looked as disturbed by the proposition as Ally felt.

'Because when Burke sees what happened to his car, he's going to murder me. Then he'll be sentenced to prison, and his life will be ruined.'

Frederick laughed. 'Gosh, for a

minute you scared me. Now what has you so upset?'

'Come with me.' Ally took his arm and led him around to the right side of the Jag. She pointed and whispered, 'Just look.'

'Oh, dear.' Frederick walked over and squatted down to look at the crumpled right rear fender.

'It wasn't my fault,' Ally gasped, trying to hold back her tears. Burke was going to hate her for sure now.

'Well, tell me. What happened?'

She shrugged helplessly. 'I don't know. I came out of Neiman-Marcus and saw it immediately. Someone must have backed into the Jag and just left! Drove off without bothering to leave their name or address!'

Frederick shook his head. 'Well, those things do happen.'

'Burke's going to kill me, isn't he?'

'No, he's not. Just explain and he'll understand.'

'But he loves this blasted car,' she said tearfully.

Frederick nodded. He wanted to tell her that Burke loved her even more, but he dared not. It was too early yet. Besides, those words needed to come from Burke.

'You could always, uh, how shall I say this delicately — withhold disclosure until another time,' he advised with a grin.

'Oh, no. I couldn't do that. That would be like lying.' Ally protested.

The decision was taken out of her hands as Burke stepped out of the front door.

'My Jag! What did you do to my Jag?' Instead of a shout, his question was an intense whisper.

Ally trembled. Then the dam of tears breached the flood gate of her control. 'I'm sorry. Oh, Burke, it's horrible. I feel terrible about this.'

Without quite knowing how it happened, Ally found herself in his arms. His hands stroked her hair as he murmured meaningless words to her. This was wonderful, she thought.

Elation swept away her misery and she savored being in his arms. Gee, if she'd known it would feel this great, she'd have crumpled that fender long before now. She sighed and snuffled.

Burke took out his handkerchief and handed it to her. He saw Tiffany exit the building and waved her away. She chose not to follow his bidding. Of course, she was still miffed at him, even though she was back to her usual businesslike demeanor.

Tiffany walked over to the Jag and bent down. 'Tsk, tsk,' she said. Her fingers stroked the new scar on the automobile. Then she looked up.

'My, my, I'm always amazed at how some women try to worm their way out of their responsibilities by shedding tears,' Tiffany said.

Ally's head jerked up. 'What did you say?'

'You heard me. I didn't whisper.'

'I'm not trying to shirk my responsibility. I'll gladly pay for the damage to Burke's car.'

'Are you sure you can afford it?'

Ally saw red. 'You're darn right I can! I could even afford to have plastic boobs like yours if I wanted them.'

'Uh, we'd better get moving,' Burke said, stepping between the two women hurriedly.

'That's okay, Burke. I'm not going to attack your pretend wife,' Tiffany smirked. 'A woman who uses tears to get her way has to insult someone she knows is smarter, better looking, and more physically appealing. It's the only way she can compete with me.'

To cap off her little speech, she leaned toward Burke and kissed him on the mouth. 'See you later, lover,' she said and patted his cheek.

Burke didn't know if he or Ally was more shocked at what his business partner had said. What had gotten into Tiff? Speechless, he watched Tiffany walk away, obviously working it. She walked and moved in a way he'd never seen before.

Ally seethed. 'So you and Tiffany are

just business partners? You were going to have a marriage of convenience? Ha!'

She was jealous! Somehow, that didn't disturb him as much as it once would have.

'I guess this means we won't be lunching together?' Burke asked. He grinned as if he were supremely happy about something. What that might be, Ally couldn't begin to guess.

* * *

Ally needed help. She'd deluded herself where Burke Winslow was concerned. Teach him how it felt to be jealous? That was a laugh. She was the one who'd been on the receiving end of that lesson today. But it wasn't too late to turn the tables. Somehow, she'd get Preston to understand how she had exaggerated their friendship into a romance. He'd play along if only because he had a heightened sense of the ridiculous.

'Preston, I need your help,' she

exclaimed when he answered the phone.

'Hey, Ally Cat. Did you change your mind about staying in Houston?'

Preston's irrepressible good humor came through the phone lines as if he were in the room.

'Oh, Preston, you remember a long time ago how you asked me to act as your personal twelve-step program? You made me promise to talk you out of it if you ever fell for a no-good bimbo again, remember?'

'Sure. But I'm between engagements, you might say.'

'I know. This is for me. Talk me out of something totally insane. Tell me I'm nuts.'

'Okay, you're nuts. Now tell me why you're nuts.'

'Well, it's Burke.'

'Uh-oh. I told you not to go down there. You should have telephoned your almost-ex.'

Ally grimaced. 'Believe me, I wish I had taken your advice. He blackmailed me into staying here, but it's a heck of a lot more difficult than I imagined it would be.'

When Preston erupted into loud laughter, Ally held the phone away from her ear. Then she said, 'Would you quit laughing? This isn't funny.'

'Oh, yes it is. The mighty Ally has fallen. Funny, I didn't hear anyone yell timber over you.'

'Preston, it's not like that. It's just . . . ' Her voice trailed off.

'Love?' Preston finished for her.

'No!' Unsettled, Ally began to pace. 'No. It isn't,' she said vehemently. 'I guess it's just lust.'

'Excuse me?' he asked.

'Don't mock me. I am twenty-four years old. I can lust if I want to.'

That really set him off to laughing. 'This I've got to see.'

'Rather than sending you a video, why don't you just come down here and witness it firsthand?'

'Yeah. I think I will. I just turned in that piece I was doing for the museum.

I think I'll take the next week and a half off and visit you.'

'Would you?'

'You mean you really want me to?' he asked, sounding surprised.

'Preston, I'll be your devoted fan forever if you'll do that.'

'Ally, are you all right?'

'It's that woman. That Tiffany he was going to marry. She's making me crazy. Kissing him right in front of me. And he tried to make me believe that she lives and breathes computer software, twenty-four-seven. It's not that I'm jealous. Well, actually it is. But I don't have any reason to be. I mean,' she babbled, 'it's not as if I have any claim on him.'

'You're his wife, aren't you?'

'Well, yes, but not really. Oh, this is so confusing. I just need someone in my corner. Will you come down here, Preston? Please say you will.'

'Sure, Ally Cat, why not? What are best friends for?'

10

Ally took special care with her appearance that evening. She decided to leave her long hair loose about her shoulders. She curled and sprayed the heavy dark tresses and spent more time than usual styling it. She studied the tousled curls and nodded. That was exactly the effect she wanted.

She intended to be on time for the dinner party, but she also intended to make Burke wait until the last possible minute to leave. Preston had told her he'd rent a car at the airport and be at Burke's house in plenty of time to make their restaurant reservation.

Actually, Preston should be ringing the doorbell any minute, she thought. She hoped she had sufficient nerve to pass him off as her lover.

She checked her appearance again in the mirror. The bright red dress swirled sexily above her knees. The shirred and gathered halter top displayed her bosom to the best advantage. All in all, it was the kind of dress that made a man look twice. She just hoped it would make Burke aware of her as a desirable woman. Maybe she could convince Preston to nuzzle her neck or gaze soulfully into her eyes.

When she couldn't stand the waiting any longer, she grabbed the red silk shoulder bag and stepped into the matching high heel sandals. Her pulse sped up in anticipation as she went downstairs. Burke was lounging on the sofa in the great room. She stopped abruptly at the foot of the stairs.

His eyes swept her from her head to her red shoes. He let out a low whistle. 'Wow.'

'Is this okay for where we are going?' she asked, knowing it was. All her preparations and primping had been worth it. She basked in the glow of his appreciation.

'I can't think of anything you'd look

better in.' He could, but he didn't think she'd be receptive to his suggesting she model his sheets, on his bed, next to him.

'You really meant you were going to make me pay through the nose,' Burke said cheerfully.

'I have a card for Neiman's,' Ally said.

'Well, I hope you didn't use it to purchase that outfit.' He liked the idea that he'd bought her clothes. He wondered if she had on red silk lingerie to match the sexy dress. The prospect of that gave him something new to fantasize about.

'If for no other reason, let's say I owe you,' Burke said. 'When we were married, I didn't have enough money to even buy you a dress at a discount store.'

'I'm glad you've done so well,' Ally said, softly, rather shyly. She felt inordinately proud of his success.

'Thanks. I can't say I did it alone. Tiffany was part of the success, as well as Dave and Craig and the others you'll meet tonight.'

'Oh, yes, Tiffany,' Ally said, feeling a twinge of jealousy at his championing the incomparable Tiffany.

The doorbell chimed. 'That's probably for me,' she said breathlessly. Suddenly, she wished that she hadn't asked Preston to come. 'I'm, uh, expecting a friend.' She had a foreboding feeling that this might do more harm than good.

Ally hurried to the door. She heard Burke behind her. When she threw open the door and saw Preston standing there, she had deep misgivings. He looked as if he'd just stepped off the cover of a men's magazine.

With jet black hair and captivating blue eyes, Preston was by far the most handsome man she'd ever known. But he still paled in comparison to Burke, she decided, seeing the two men together for the first time.

'Hey, Ally Cat,' Preston said, giving her his devil-may-care grin. She looked over her shoulder and met Burke's stormy eyes, realizing that she'd made a serious error in judgment.

Ally embraced him as she would have any friend. 'Preston, how nice of you to come.'

'Ally! Darling!' Preston pulled her into his arms and planted a kiss on her. Then his eyes opened. Ally went cross-eyed looking into his baby blues. He winked. He proceeded to ignore Ally's pleading face.

'What's going on here?' Burke demanded.

Ally looked over her shoulder at him. His face looked like a thundercloud.

Ally took Preston's arm and pulled him into the house. 'Oh, Burke, this is Preston Kesey. My friend. From Dallas.' What had she done?

'Hey,' Preston said, extending his hand.

Burke eyed his hand as if it held some exotic poison. Then he took it and did his best to mangle it. Unfortunately, Ally's friend was stronger than he looked. Burke grunted and broke the contact.

'Nice to meet you, Winslow,' Preston said.

Burke grunted in reply. 'Yeah. Same here, Pesto.'

'Preston,' Ally corrected. 'I called Preston today to ask him to take care of my apartment. We, um, got to talking, and one thing led to another, and here he is,' she finished with a bright smile.

'Yeah,' Preston said. 'You know how it is. We just couldn't stand to be away from each other.' He brushed a kiss against Ally's cheek but she jerked and he ended up with a mouthful of hair.

'Get your hands — and your mouth — off my wife!' Burke snapped.

Preston grinned lazily. 'Hey, be cool, man. She might be your wife, but she's my girlfriend.'

That pronouncement made matters worse. Ally jumped into the breach. 'Now, Burke, you wouldn't begrudge me a friend of my own, would you? After all, you've got Dave, and Craig, and your brother, and Tiffany.'

Tiffany!

So that's what this was about. He should have known, Burke thought. She must have come straight home and called old Piston to come down here. Why that sly, conniving . . . So she wanted to play games, huh?

Burke would be nice if it killed him. It shouldn't be that difficult now that he knew the game he was expected to play.

'Forgive me. I didn't realize at first who you were. You're her special friend from Dallas, aren't you?'

'Special friend?' Preston repeated. His eyes laughed at Ally. He reached out and caught a lock of hair and curled it around his finger. 'Yeah, I guess I am. Not too many friends would go to such lengths, would they, Ally Cat?'

Her eyes promised him that she would get him back for this.

'So we're supposed to go to dinner, aren't we?' he asked.

Burke was tempted to say that *he*

wasn't invited. 'Yes, we are, Piston. Did you come in a rental car?'

'That's Preston,' Ally said. Preston just grinned and nodded at Burke as if he found something amusing.

Burke scowled. 'Well, just leave it out front. We'll take what's left of my Jag. You and Ally can squeeze together up front and catch up on the last few days you've been apart. This should be a great evening!'

Burke was torn between amusement and jealousy. On the one hand, he thought Ally's transparent scheme was hilarious. On the other, he didn't appreciate that overdressed lounge lizard mauling her in front of him.

Ally had never had a more uncomfortable thirty minutes in her life than the half hour it took to get from Burke's house to the restaurant. She sat crushed between the two large men, scared to death that Preston would say something to give away her ruse. But Preston had performed like a trouper. If anything, he had played his role a little too well.

Burke looked as if he had a severe case of indigestion by the time he handed the Jag's keys to the valet at the popular Mexican restaurant. 'Don't bother being careful with it,' he muttered.

The restaurant looked like Hollywood's version of a 1930's Mexican village. Colored lights outlined the roof. Faded murals and advertisements adorned the artistically patched stucco walls. Cactus and huge pots of begonias and petunias dotted the courtyard.

A mariachi band added to the noise level, but Ally didn't mind. If it were really noisy, maybe she wouldn't have to make conversation with Preston. She knew her friend was going to tease her mercilessly about this.

Her brow wrinkled. She tried to remember back to the night at the church. Why had she thought it necessary to convince Burke that she had a lover? It was his fault, she decided, irritated at the ridiculous situation in which she found herself.

The manager of the restaurant led them to the back where tables had been set up. Ally walked between Burke and Preston, feeling as if she were a prisoner being escorted to her last meal.

Ally looked at the people lining the tables and cried, 'Granny! What are you doing here?'

'Your nice young man invited me,' the attractive silver-haired woman said. She turned to Frederick Winslow and smiled. 'Your grandson is so thoughtful.'

'Yep,' Frederick agreed. 'Like grandfather, like grandson.'

'Mrs. Fletcher, it's wonderful to see you again. I'm so glad you could come,' Burke said. He held Ally's chair, but Preston had pulled one out also.

Ally looked at the two chairs and it occurred to her that it was going to be a long, long evening.

11

The evening turned out to be one of the most frustrating that Ally had ever spent. On the one hand, she loved being there with people she cared about but hadn't seen much of in recent years, like her grandmother, Burke's grandfather, Rod, Dave, and Craig. Even Burke, she thought grudgingly.

On the other hand, by the time she'd finished her fajitas, she was ready to do violence to her husband-in-name-only. He had spent the evening ignoring her and playing up to Tiffany. She'd never seen him act so . . . so revoltingly romantic.

The first time he'd leaned toward Tiffany and whispered with his mouth a half inch from the woman's ear, Ally had wanted to jerk him away from her. She'd had to get used to the intimate laughs Burke and Tiffany had shared

— the whispers they'd exchanged. She was sick of watching him murmur sweet nothings in the woman's ear.

Tiffany's laughter grated on her nerves. Each time she laughed, she covered her mouth as if to suppress it, then she would smile encouragingly at Burke. She welcomed his attentions. Obviously, they had kissed and made up after the debacle at the church. In fact, Ally guessed she was witnessing their making up. Whoopee, she thought sourly. Lucky me!

It was totally disgusting, she decided, leaning over quickly as if she'd dropped her napkin. Her maneuver successfully eluded Preston's lips. During the long evening, she'd developed radar where her friend was concerned. It was a toss-up as to which man was being the most infuriating — Burke with his open flirtation or Preston who seemed determined to treat Ally to the same romantic attention that Burke was bestowing on Tiffany.

To think she had worried about being

able to persuade Preston to act lover-like. Heck, if he acted any more lover-like, she'd sue him for sexual harassment.

Just then Preston's head popped down next to hers. 'We've got to stop meeting like this,' he said, grinning like an idiot.

'I thought I dropped my napkin,' Ally said.

'Guess not, huh?'

Ally started to raise up but Preston stopped her with a hand on her arm. 'Say, Ally Cat, what's the story on Tiffany?'

'What do you mean?'

'Is she truly spoken for?'

'Draw your own conclusion. My husband can't seem to keep his hands off her.'

Preston grinned. 'Yeah. I noticed. Good.'

'Good? I'd say it's disgusting and revolting.'

Ally heard a chair scrape on the ceramic tile and then Burke's head joined hers and Preston's near the floor.

'What's going on here?' Burke asked.

'Ally Cat just wanted a private word with me, Bark,' Preston said.

'The name is Burke, Percy.'

'Oh, right, right. Well, if you two will excuse me, all the blood's rushing to my head. I think I'll just walk around and get acquainted with the other guests.' Preston raised up and scooted his chair back.

'Ally Cat, huh?' Burke huffed. 'And just how did you get that nickname?'

'Use your imagination,' Ally said nastily.

She sat up again and drew a deep breath. She saw that Preston had walked over to chat with Rod.

Burke rose and turned back to Tiffany. Ally tried not to watch, but this time, he didn't touch her or talk to her. Instead, he talked across her to his grandfather.

Ally tried to ignore him. She chatted with her grandmother across the table. Granny Edith seemed to be having a great time. She'd laughed and talked with Frederick much of the evening, Ally had noticed.

Ally heard Burke make a comment about the upcoming vacation that Frederick had scheduled.

'Oh, Granddad,' Ally said, 'You're going on a cruise too?'

At his nod, she said, 'So is my grandmother. She went on one last year and had a ball.'

'Granddad went on one last year too,' Burke said. 'Where did you go, Mrs. Fletcher?'

Edith Fletcher waved her hand. 'Oh, just one of those package deals. I forget the places we stopped.'

'But didn't you say you had so much fun you were booking the same one this year?' Ally asked. Then, to her amazement, Granny blushed. She didn't think she'd ever seen her grandmother blush before. To her further surprise, the woman said, 'Oh, dear me, it's way past my bedtime. I think I need to be going.' She thanked Burke, said her goodbyes and left.

Ally looked at her watch. It wasn't quite ten o'clock. She'd never known Granny Edith to go to bed before one in the morning. It was a standing joke — she was the night owl of the family.

After a few minutes, Frederick stood. 'I think I'll follow suit. This party is for you young people. And an old codger like me needs to be in bed to get my beauty sleep.'

Burke watched him leave. 'I'm worried about him, Rod,' he said across the table.

'Do you think he feels all right?' Ally asked, concerned also.

'I think he feels too good,' Rod said, chuckling.

'What do you mean?' Burke asked.

'I mean, he's in love,' Rod said with a satisfied grin.

'No!' Burke scoffed. 'What ever gave you that idea?'

'Because I walked into the kitchen yesterday and overheard him on the phone. He was making a late date for tonight. He may be headed to bed, but not necessarily his own. If you get my drift.'

'Well, I'll be damned.' Burke whistled low. 'That sly old dog.' He looked up at Rod. 'Do you know who she is?'

'Nope. And he's not telling. He told me to mind my p's and q's and keep my mouth shut.'

Ally wished her grandmother could find someone like Frederick. Granny Edith had been alone since Ally was a child. She started to say something, but her attention was distracted by Preston who had made his way around the table and now settled into the chair next to Tiffany. Her mouth snapped closed.

What was it about that woman that drew every man? Sure, she was beautiful and built, Ally thought resentfully, but did Preston have to fall for her also?

Everyone seemed paired off in close conversations. Only she and Burke were at loose ends. Looking around, she decided that she liked this disparate group that composed Byte Me's executive corps. It was an interesting mix of men and women of all ages — some younger than Burke, some older. They appeared to be the brightest in terms of computer application and design, from what she'd heard discussed at the table.

To a person, they'd accepted her at face value as if there were nothing out of the ordinary about a wife who popped up after a six-year absence.

Judging by the wide grins, she figured the story of her appearance at Burke's wedding had made the rounds.

★　★　★

'So tell me, Tiffany, how did you get mixed up with this bunch of maniacs?' Preston asked.

Tiffany stared into his eyes and found herself unable to form a coherent thought. She'd sat, mesmerized by him from the moment he'd walked in and been introduced to the group. She'd never met anyone before who made her heart beat so fast that she was certain she'd have a heart attack if it didn't slow.

Never comfortable with small talk, she usually discussed business — either her own or the business world in general. But at the moment, she couldn't think of anything to say.

Preston hadn't blinked as he looked into her eyes, as green as new leaves on a spring morning. She was perfect in every way, in his opinion. Something about her had him acting bolder than he ever had with a woman he'd just met. He reached out and touched her hand. Sliding his fingers up the soft skin, he encircled her wrist, and felt the wild pulse pounding there. It told him all he needed to know.

'I think you and I have a lot in common,' he said, feeling his own response to her nearness.

Tiffany studied his mouth and wondered how it would feel next to hers. She'd never had a thought like that before in all her twenty-six years.

'I have an MBA in finance, and I'm

the co-owner of this computer software company,' she said breathlessly.

Preston's eyes dropped to her lips. He caressed them with his eyes, imagined wetting them with his tongue before sliding it into her delectable mouth.

'I have a degree in fine art. I paint brilliant master-pieces that seldom sell.'

Tiffany moved, ever so slightly toward him. 'You're right,' she murmured, 'we do have a lot in common.'

* * *

The waitress appeared to take drink refill orders.

'Hang the instant fat,' Ally told her. 'I'll have another frozen margarita. No salt.'

'What do you mean, instant fat?' Burke asked as soon as the waitress moved on.

Ally was a little embarrassed that he had heard. She shrugged. 'I usually limit myself to one drink. Alcohol is in that category of instant fat that I can generally do without.'

'Since when do you worry about calories? You've never had a weight problem.'

Ally laughed. 'That shows how little you know about me.'

He turned his chair and gave her his full attention. 'So tell me something I don't know,' he challenged her.

'All right. I will. Until my senior year in high school, I was fat.'

'Get out of town!' Burke's expression said as clearly as his words that he didn't believe her.

'It's true,' Ally insisted.

The waitress set their drinks in front of them. Each picked up the iced mug. Burke lifted his in salute. 'To a successful conclusion to this deal,' he toasted.

Ally clicked her mug next to his. Her idea of a successful conclusion was undergoing a radical change. But that was her own fault for seeking him out. She sucked on the straw, drawing the delicious frozen concoction into her mouth. 'This is wonderful. I love that salty, limey taste.' She picked up the wedge of lime from the mug and bit into it. Then she licked the drops of lime juice from her lips.

Burke thought he wouldn't be able to control himself. He wanted to taste that lime wedge too — from her tongue.

'So tell me, if you were fat, how come you were thin as a rail when we met?' he managed to ask.

'Before my senior year, I decided that I was tired of being Elaine's four-eyed, chubby little sister. Elaine was always so gorgeous and so smart. I wasn't anything like that.'

'I never got a chance to meet your sister, but I find it difficult to believe you didn't outshine her.'

His praise warmed her. Or was it the effects of the alcohol? 'Elaine never comes home much. She's been in Paris going on eight years now.'

'She couldn't possibly hold a candle to you.'

'I swear it's true. I went on a diet before school started and started jogging. I hated running, though. So I decided to just cut calories until I lost the weight. By graduation I had done it, mostly by willpower and starvation.'

'Isn't that bad for the body?' He frowned.

'It is. You lose weight, but then you tend to regain it immediately. In my case, I was so paranoid about staying thin, that I did stupid things to keep the weight off. Believe me, you don't want to know.'

'But you're still not doing that, are you?' He seemed worried.

'No. Fortunately, after we split up, I came to my senses. It took a long time, but I learned to eat healthy foods and most importantly, I learned to love exercise.' She looked down, embarrassed.

'Funny. When I quit starving myself and started living a healthy lifestyle, I stopped seeing myself as a fat girl. Before that, every time I looked in the mirror, that was what I saw.' She wanted to tell him that was the source of all her insecurities, but she couldn't bring herself to bare her naked soul to him.

'I just can't picture you that way. When I saw you on the beach that day we met . . . Wow! You took my breath away.'

Ally wanted to tell him that was how she had felt too.

'I guess you're one of those diet success stories. You never gained the weight back?'

'I tried when we first divorced,' Ally confessed.

'How?'

'I pigged out or tried to, but I had lost my fondness for bingeing. I have put a few pounds on over the years, but I think that's because I have more muscle now.'

'And it looks great on you,' Burke said, warmly.

Ally was nonplussed by his compliment. 'Thank you,' she said. Ally could have kissed him. His words meant a lot to her.

Burke leaned toward her. He reached out and laid the palm of his hand on her cheek. 'Beautiful Ally,' he said.

'Hey, Brick, get your hands off my woman,' Preston said from behind them.

Ally jumped. Burke stiffened. 'Who says she's your woman?'

'Why, she does! That's why she called and asked me down here. She was lonesome for me.' He winked. 'Know what I mean?'

Ally wanted to strangle Preston. The man's timing was abominable. She was going to have to talk to him about this lover act of his.

'Oh, I know exactly what you mean,' Burke said. He'd like to strangle the man. He didn't care, though. Let Ally have her fling with this jerk. He'd show her. He stood and dug in his pants pocket for his keys. He tossed them down in front of Ally.

'Why don't you take the Jag home and take Piercey back to his car. I'll get

Tiffany to drop me off after . . . ' His voice trailed off suggestively.

Ally turned to Preston with a smile so briliant it hurt her face. 'Great idea. Let's go now, Preston, so we'll have the rest of the evening together.'

'Whatever you say, Ally Cat.'

Burke ground his teeth together. He hated that man calling his wife that revolting nickname.

'Fine,' Burke said, standing. He pulled Tiffany's chair out.

'What — ' Tiffany sputtered, spilling the drink she'd been sipping when Burke had suddenly jerked her chair backwards.

★ ★ ★

Frederick's lover welcomed him when he arrived. He took the glass of red wine she offered him. He leaned back on her couch and sighed.

'Tired?' she asked softly.

He lifted her hand. 'It is a bit of a drive down here.'

'But I'm worth it. Right?' she teased.

'Absolutely.' He sipped the wine. His eyes never left her dark ones.

'So how do you think it's going?' He asked.

Her brow wrinkled. 'I don't know, Freddy. I'm beginning to wonder if this was a good idea.'

'Don't wonder. This was the best idea I ever had. Those two belong together. I know my grandson. I know what he went through after they split up. He needs her. This will work.'

She laughed. 'If you say so.'

'Well, that and some good sex will do the trick.' He grinned, his eyes brightening. He stroked her hair.

'Speaking of that . . . ' He lifted his brows questioningly.

'I thought you were tired,' she said, smiling.

'Darlin', I'm never too tired for that.'

'Men!' she said in mock disgust, throwing her arms around him.

* * *

'I cannot believe the nerve of that teenage Romeo,' Burke seethed, fiddling with the radio dial.

'Who are you talking about?' Tiffany asked, braking for the turn into Burke's subdivision.

'Ally's boyfriend, that's who!' Burke snapped the radio off.

'He's not a teenager.'

'She's old enough to be his . . . his older sister.'

'And I'm a couple of years older than Ally,' Tiffany said with a doleful sigh.

'What's that got to do with anything?' Burke asked. Without waiting for an answer, he ranted, 'The way they were whispering and nuzzling each other at the table turned my stomach. Can't they wait until they get behind closed doors to carry on like that?'

'Did I misunderstand?' Tiffany asked softly.

'What does she see in that kid?' Burke asked, ignoring Tiffany's plaintive question.

'Maybe if your wife hadn't encouraged

him, then he wouldn't have behaved so outrageously. A woman sets the tone of a relationship. I'd say your wife plays fast and loose.'

'Tiffany, did I ever tell you that you talk too much?'

★   ★   ★

'Did you see the way Tiffany acted?' Ally demanded, grinding the gears of the Jag as she shifted into high.

Preston winced. 'Those things aren't made of rubber, Ally. Take it easy on the poor car.'

Ally withered him with a glance. 'And you! How do you explain yourself, mister?'

'What do you mean?' Preston asked. 'I was just playing up to you to make your husband or whatever he is jealous. That is what you really wanted me here for, isn't it?'

'I don't mean that charade. I mean you fawning all over Tiffany. Isn't it enough that she has Burke wound around her little finger without my best friend falling for her too?'

Preston laughed. 'Let's put a little perspective to this picture. What has you most upset? Me flirting with Tiffany or Burke flirting with her all night?'

'To think he tried to convince me that his wedding to her was a marriage of convenience.' She down-shifted, and the engine roared in protest.

'I don't know who I feel sorrier for,' Preston said. 'You or this poor car.'

12

Ally watched Preston drive away in the convertible Mustang. At least he'd had the good fortune to get a decent car at the rental agency. Maybe if she'd been equally lucky, she wouldn't be in this pickle now. She turned to go, but paused when headlights swung into the driveway.

Oh, no. Burke. And Tiffany. She hoped they hadn't seen her. She dashed inside, not wanting to witness their goodnight kiss — or something even worse.

Maybe if she stayed in her room and didn't see Burke again until the night of the Sakamoto party, she'd be able to keep her dignity intact. She didn't want him to realize that she had fallen victim to the green-eyed monster once again. At the moment, she felt more jealous than she'd ever been. Maybe because that was because she wanted him more than she'd ever thought possible.

The only thing that saved her was that he hadn't tried to seduce her. Except for this morning when she'd surprised him by the bed, he'd seemed completely immune to whatever had once drawn them together. She didn't understand how that was possible. It hurt her ego that he hadn't once tried anything with her. Was she *that* undesirable?

'Face it, Ally Fletcher,' she muttered as she climbed the stairs to her room. 'You're miserable around him and miserable away from him. In short, you're just a mess.'

Exhausted, Ally decided on a shower and bed. That was better than listening for the murmur of voices from downstairs. She didn't want to know what was going on in the great room, or worse yet, in Burke's luxurious master suite.

Unfortunately, two hours later, Ally still found herself tossing and turning.

The warm shower hadn't helped. Counting sheep wasn't effective — they all turned into randy goats! Maybe a glass of milk would do the trick, she thought, tossing the covers back.

* ★ *

Burke lifted the jug of milk from the refrigerator just as the light in the kitchen flickered on.

'Oh, I didn't know you were up,' Ally said, tightening the belt of her crinkle-cotton robe. Her pulse leaped at the sight of Burke, clad only in a pair of jeans. His feet were bare. So was his chest, she thought, her eyes feasting on the expanse of tanned skin. When she became aware that he noticed her gaze, she looked away immediately.

'I was thirsty,' he said. 'Thought I'd get some milk. Want some?'

Ally swallowed. She certainly did want some. 'Milk? Sure,' she said, in a rush. Her face reddened. She hoped he didn't notice. They both turned and

186

reached for a glass at the same time. His arm brushed across her breasts.

She jumped back.

'Sorry,' he mumbled.

'No problem.' She retied her belt again, pulling the sash so tight it hurt. Darn her blasted hormones!

Burke filled two glasses and handed her one along with a paper napkin.

'Thanks.' She should go back to her room, she thought. Instead, she pulled out a chair at the breakfast table and sat down, ignoring her own common sense.

Burke joined her at the table. He wiped his suddenly clammy hands on his jeans. He was afraid to open his mouth for fear he'd ask her to join him in bed. The silence was so deep he figured she could hear him swallow as he gulped his milk.

Ally watched Burke's throat as he swallowed. Her eyes slid down his throat to his shoulders. She loved his shoulders. Looking at him made her tingle in places that hadn't tingled in an awfully long time.

She turned her glass of milk around and around. She didn't want it. She wanted the feel of his mouth on hers, his hands on her body, the sensation of his skin beneath her hands.

'Whew!' Ally picked up the napkin and blotted her forehead. 'It's warm in here.'

'Now that you mention it, you're right.' Burke grabbed his napkin and blotted his forehead. 'Why don't we step out onto the patio? It's always cool at night out by the pool.'

'Sounds good,' Ally said.

Burke led her through the great room, his mind working fast as he thought of a new scheme. When they got to the hallway that led to his bedroom, Ally halted.

'Can't we go out through the French doors in the great room?'

'I've got the alarm set for those, but it's bypassed for the ones in my bedroom,' he explained.

'Oh. Okay.'

She bought it. Relieved, he flipped on

188

the lights in the hallway. He knew he couldn't impress her with his etchings, he mused. She hadn't liked the contemporary artwork he'd spent so much money on one bit. Maybe his body would do the trick.

They entered his bedroom. After one quick glance at the massive bed with its rumpled covers, Ally averted her eyes. She was having enough trouble with her wayward thoughts without that stimulus. She needed to fight this attraction. But she was so weak, and he was so magnetic.

'Hey, want to go swimming?' Burke asked.

'I don't have a suit.'

'So?' He arched one brow, giving him a decidedly rakish expression.

Ally inhaled quickly. 'I think I should go back to my own bed.'

'Why? What's the matter? Are you afraid you can't control your impulses?'

Ally stiffened. 'I don't have any trouble controlling mine,' she lied. 'I just don't want you thinking that we're going to engage in any hanky panky.'

'Hanky panky?' He hooted. 'That sounds like a phrase our grandparents would use.'

He didn't fool Ally. She suddenly sensed the real reason he had lured her to his room. And it wasn't to exit from the French doors in here. She shook all over. With indignation, she told herself. Not with longing.

'Burke Winslow, I have a news flash for you. I am not sleeping with you.'

Burke felt his control slip a notch. She didn't seem to have a problem being overly-friendly with that Pearsall guy. 'Well, I have a flash for you, Ally Cat. I didn't ask you to.'

'Good. Because I'm not.' Somehow, she didn't feel as triumphant as she should. His flat refusal bothered her. 'But in case I was interested, which I'm not, why do you say no?' She walked over to the wall and flipped one of the switches. Lights came on beyond the pool, highlighting the towering trees in back.

Burke walked over to where she stood and flipped another switch. Suddenly lights inside the pool glowed, turning it into a sparkling jewel.

'Oh, beautiful,' Ally said.

'As I recall,' Burke said, 'when we were married, we didn't exactly burn up the sheets.' There was more than one way to skin a cat, Burke decided slyly.

His words annoyed Ally. She flipped another switch. Soft music poured from hidden speakers. A haunting, sensual horn saxophone solo swirled through the room. Great. This was just what she needed, she thought, suddenly realizing how precarious her emotions were. She started to flip that switch off, but Burke's hand covered hers.

'Leave it,' he said softly.

Ally's heart pounded so hard, she was certain he could hear it. Her breathing became ragged.

'Funny,' she said, unable to resist his challenge. She dashed foolhardily into trouble. 'I remember it differently. You couldn't keep your hands off me.'

Burke reached out and touched the curve of her cheek with his index finger. He stroked down the smooth skin. 'Poor Ally. You must have amnesia. You and I just didn't click when it came to sex.' His finger continued down her throat and stopped at the barrier of her robe.

Ally imitated his gesture except she didn't stop the movement of her finger at his throat. She continued, her finger moving slowly, every nerve cell in the tip of it tingling with desire as she traced a line from his cheek to his chest, over the pebbled nipple and down to the low-slung waist of his jeans.

She knew she was playing with fire, but she couldn't stop herself. 'Perhaps you're the one with the selective memory.'

Burke groaned and gasped, 'In your dreams, sweetheart.' He sucked in his breath, and his jeans loosened revealing his taut belly. Ally's finger moved into the slight space and stopped.

He wasn't wearing any underwear, she realized.

Her heart beat painfully hard and she spoke with great effort. The words came out low, husky with want. 'Not my dreams, baby,' she teased.

She could hardly stand, her knees trembled so. Her body felt as if she were going up in flames. She leaned her forehead against his chest. She trembled. 'I don't lose any sleep dreaming about you and me in bed.'

'Your bed or my bed?' he asked, gasping.

'Yours. It's closer.' She untied her robe and flung it aside.

'Oh, Ally!' Burke gathered her into his arms and kissed her like she'd never been kissed before. He lifted her and carried her over to the huge bed, setting her down carefully in the center as if she were a porcelain doll who would break.

Then his control shattered. Ally felt as if she were caught in a whirlwind.

Her gown vanished as quickly as his jeans, and then, finally, she had what she wanted — his body next to hers.

His touch was all that she remembered. His kisses took her breath away.

Ally rolled over and assumed the superior position, guiding him and telling him what she wanted.

'Your wish is my command,' Burke whispered, delighting in this new Ally. He gloried in her possession of him. Though he had lied in saying they hadn't had great sex when they'd been married, it had been nothing like this.

Ally had always been hesitant, he suddenly realized. Now she was an equal partner. This was better than before. His wife had become one formidable force to deal with.

What had made her so aggressive in bed? He frowned. He didn't like the name that popped into his head.

Ally kissed his frown away. She moved urgently, afraid she'd awake before this dream reached its climax.

Then she cried out suddenly. Burke

watched her body convulse, satisfied that he had given her this. Then he gave in to his own release.

Ally collapsed across him. He kissed the damp tendrils of hair away from her face.

Ally pressed her face into his chest. Too horrified by what had happened to face him, she hid. She'd known what he was doing. Why had she fallen into his clutches? Fallen? the small voice of her conscience whispered. She hadn't fallen. She'd flung herself headlong.

What about Tiffany? that same conscience whispered. Ally moved restlessly. He's *my* husband, she answered back. Not hers. If I have my way, then he'll stay my husband. The thought suddenly exhilarated her.

Ally felt his hands stroking up her sides and around to her back. She should leave. She really should. But she didn't want to. She wanted to stay with him. Woo him. Win him.

His hands stole away what little will she had left. This time he set the pace.

Ally thought she'd go stark raving mad. He turned until she lay on the mattress, her eyes gazing into his. She beat her fists against his back, but he took his time. And Ally loved every agonizing minute of it.

When he couldn't stand it any longer, he groaned and yielded to her pleas, giving her every pleasure she begged for and more.

Exhausted, he collapsed next to her. He pulled her against his side and mumbled, 'Bet Percy can't top that.'

After a few minutes, his words soaked into her besotted brain. Ally's eyes flew open. Burke snored gently next to her.

Oh! How could he? She'd never forgive him for this, Ally thought, freeing herself from his arms. Quickly she found her gown and slipped it on. She grabbed her robe and ran to the guest room.

How could Burke have been so callous? He'd only made love to her to get back at Preston!

13

Ally slept little that night. Instead, she played the scene over and over in her mind. Maybe she had misjudged Burke. Maybe she should give him a chance to apologize or explain.

Exhausted, she fell asleep shortly before dawn. By the time she crawled out of bed the next morning, the sun had reached its zenith.

Ally took care to hide the dark circles under her eyes and make herself presentable. When she finally gathered the courage to go downstairs and confront the tight-lipped housekeeper, she was told that Burke wouldn't be home for dinner that evening.

Hurt, Ally still hung around the house, thinking he might call. The hours crawled by at a snail's pace. She camped on the huge sectional sofa in the great room and dolefully channel surfed, not paying attention to any of the banal television programs.

By midnight, she was in a black mood. He'd had his chance. He'd chosen not to use it.

Her hurt grew during the following days.

Ally avoided Burke as much as possible for the next week. She took the Jag out each day, finding pleasure in driving the magnificent machine. Burke had never asked for his keys back, and she hadn't offered them.

In fact, he hadn't sought her out at all. She chafed at the fact that he still had made no effort to apologize for how he'd ruined their beautiful evening together. She tried to convince herself that she didn't care, but she did. She cared so much that she thought her heart would break each time she thought of him.

She'd been right. A marriage in name only between the two of them couldn't work. Somehow that affirmation did little to comfort her.

This was so much worse than before. She spent her days trying to figure out why that was. She finally came to the conclusion that it was because she was mature enough now to know what real love felt like — and suffered from an acute case of it.

Ally just couldn't continue playing the game of making him jealous with poor Preston. She'd planned to tell Preston that, but suddenly he seemed to be avoiding her also. That was too bad. He could have cheered her up, she thought.

The day before the big party for Sakamoto, she drove down to Galveston to visit her grandmother. By now, she could shift the Jag with ease. She stomped the accelerator, wishing it were Burke's foot. Maybe a sharp pain there would wake him up and make him come to his senses.

She sped over the causeway that separated Galveston Island from the Texas mainland. The hot, sunny day brought back memories of her trip to Galveston the summer she'd met

Burke. Growing up in Dallas, she'd spent most of her summers with her dad's mother in Galveston. She hadn't returned since that fateful summer she had fallen in love with Burke.

Slowing, she negotiated the traffic on the main thoroughfare that led into the city. Her mind was so full of memories and regrets that she couldn't appreciate the lush stand of red-blossomed oleanders growing on the wide boulevard.

She turned onto the street that led to what was known as the Silk Stocking District, several square blocks filled with old mansions and Victorian-style homes, some of which had survived the killer hurricane of 1900.

Ally made another turn and pulled into a narrow driveway bordered by old-fashioned yellow day lilies in full bloom. Emotion clogged her throat as she saw the creamy white clapboard house with its ginger-bread painted a deep green. She'd always loved Granny Edith's island home.

As she got out of the car, her

grandmother opened the front door and stepped out onto the porch.

Ally took one look at her and crumpled. 'Oh, Granny,' she cried, dashing up the steps and throwing herself into her grandmother's arms.

'Why, child, what's wrong?' Her grandmother patted her back just as she had when Ally had been little and had turned to her for comfort.

'Everything.' Ally snuffled loudly. 'I can't think of a thing that's right.'

'Oh, dear.' Edith Fletcher said. 'Let's sit here on the porch, and you can tell me all about it. I made a nice banana bread this morning when you called. I'll get us some of that and some Earl Grey tea. That will help you put everything in perspective.'

She steered Ally over to the wicker rocker and gently pushed her into it. Then she tipped the chair back and set it rocking.

'I find gentle rocking and good tea will cure most of life's ills.' She tipped Ally's chin up and smiled at her.

Ally returned her smile. 'I hope you're right.'

While Granny puttered in the kitchen, Ally closed her eyes and used her feet to keep the chair rocking. The motion did soothe her. The balmy day relaxed her tense muscles. She could smell old-fashioned scented petunias and the oleander that grew between the yards on this block.

After a while, Edith came back with a tray. 'Here we go.' She set the tray on the small wicker table in front of a settee and proceeded to pour two cups of fragrant tea.

'I'm not really hungry,' Ally said.

Edith chuckled. 'I guess you have grown up, Ally. I remember when you were little, the first thing you wanted to do when you got hurt was eat.'

Ally grimaced. 'Luckily, I outgrew that habit or I would be as big as the side of a barn.'

'I always told you maturity and hormones would take care of your baby fat.'

At that Ally had to laugh. 'That and

eating a healthy diet, not to mention learning to like sweating.'

'I'm sure that helped a little.'

Ally took the small plate of banana bread. 'This really is good, Granny,' she said after taking a small bite. Then she set it aside.

'Okay, now tell me. What's your problem? Is it that husband of yours?'

'He's not my husband!'

'I have evidence to the contrary,' Edith said. 'Just a minute.' She went into the house but soon returned with a sheaf of papers bound in a blue cover.

'So that's what started this whole disaster.'

'Now, Ally, don't be bitter.' Edith handed them to her.

'It's weird how these turned up on the same day that Burke was getting married,' Allie mused.

'Oh!' Edith choked and coughed.

'Are you all right?'

Edith nodded, her face very red. 'Yes, just went down the wrong way I guess.' Quickly, she changed the subject. 'What are you wearing to the big party tomorrow night?'

Ally shrugged. 'I don't know. I had this knock-out dress, but I don't see much point in wearing it now. There's no one who cares.'

'What about Burke? Doesn't he care?'

'I doubt it. He only cares about making that deal.' She looked away, blinking back the tears. 'And about being the big dog on the porch,' she muttered.

'What was that, dear? About dogs?' Edith asked, confused.

'Oh, nothing. I'm just rambling.'

'I think you might be wrong about Burke not caring,' Edith said shrewdly. 'Maybe the problem is that you can't see his side of this.'

Ally bit her lower lip. 'You're wrong. I do see his side. I guess the biggest problem is that I want to be the number one priority in his life. I care too much. He just doesn't have room in his life for anything other than that damned company of his. He's just using me to get that business deal through. Well, I won't be used, Granny.'

'I'm sure that's not true. Burke cares for you, Ally. I think these two weeks have been a rare opportunity for each of you to see what you lost when you walked out. And you were the one to walk out on him, child.'

Ally nodded miserably. 'I know. I know. You don't know how many times I've regretted that night. I thought if I could just do it over that I'd get it right. But I've had my chance and I blew it. Maybe we're both still too immature.' She laughed bitterly. 'Maybe we should just try again in another six years.'

'Somehow I don't think a man like Burke Winslow will be on the marriage market in another six years.' Edith said.

'You're right,' Ally whispered. 'I knew this was my last chance, and I blew it. I did something I should never have done. Wow! I've screwed up just as badly as before.'

'What on earth did you do that was

so bad?' Edith asked.

Ally blushed hotly. She couldn't tell her grandmother about her night of passion.

'Oh, I see,' Edith said. 'Well,' she hesitated, 'did the earth not move?'

Ally choked on a laugh. 'Granny!'

'I may be your grandmother, but I do know how important s-e-x is to a relationship,' she said primly. 'So it was nothing to write home about,' she added.

'No! That's not true.' Ally dropped her head. 'It was better than before,' she whispered.

'Well, that's because you are both older. Trust me, dear, sex when you're young is nothing compared to sex when you're older.'

'Granny!' Ally was shocked. She'd never heard her grandmother speak so frankly.

Edith continued, 'You were nothing but kids when you married.' She sighed. 'I always felt responsible for what happened. If you hadn't been staying with me that summer, you'd never have met Burke.'

'Why, Granny, I didn't know you felt that way.'

'Well, I do. I'd do anything to make it right, Ally. I know your mother and Frank have always blamed me. I thought my son would disown me after you and Burke announced you were getting married. My, but he was upset.'

'Then why didn't he and Mom put up a bigger fuss about it?' Ally asked.

Edith smiled. 'I asked him the same thing. He said he took one look at your young man and saw himself when he'd first met your mother.'

'I never knew that,' Ally said, marveling at that bit of information. She rolled her eyes. 'Can you imagine what they're going to say when they find out about this fiasco?'

'Well, if nothing comes of this — '

'And it won't!' Ally interrupted.

'Then I don't see any reason to tell them anything,' Edith said. 'I'll keep it quiet if you will.'

'Oh, Granny, you're the best.'

'I just wish old age had brought more

wisdom,' Edith said with a fond smile. 'It's so hard to know if you're doing the right thing when you meddle.'

'You're not meddling,' Ally said, reaching over and hugging her.

'Then let me not meddle some more and ask you this. If you think Tiffany has Burke wrapped around her little finger, what are you doing to unwrap him?'

'What do you mean?'

'Well, in my day, if a woman wanted a man, she went after him. As near as I can see, you have a prior claim on your man. Are you just going to hand him over without a fight?'

'But you don't understand. He doesn't want me. I don't think he even wants Tiffany. I think she really is just a business associate,' Ally said earnestly. 'I'd almost be happy for him if he did want Tiffany. I don't like to think of him growing older without someone to love him.' Tears spilled over her eyes.

Edith brushed Ally's tousled hair away from her forehead. 'You're very wise, child. Men who are married to their businesses often end up lonely. And sometimes it's too late when they finally realize what they sacrificed.'

'I don't want that to happen to Burke,' Ally whispered.

'Then fight for him.'

'But how? How do you take a man away from what he loves? That business of his means more to him than anything else in his life. I just don't know what to do!'

'Are you sure about that? Let me give you something to think about. It takes two to tango.'

Ally waited. Finally she said, 'It takes to tango, and . . . ?' She lifted her brows in question.

'That's all. Just think about that. If you got something from the other night that was worth writing home about, what about him?'

Ally felt the color flood her face again.

'Just think about it, dear.' Her grandmother lifted the teapot. 'More tea before you go?'

14

By tonight it would all be over, Burke thought, studying his reflection in the mirror. The caterer had arrived with the serving staff, and delectable odors wafted through the busy house. The last time he'd gone to check on their progress, he'd seen that everything was ready.

Silver serving dishes glittered on the buffet. Sparkling crystal waited for the bartender. Fresh flowers filled every room. Even Deirdre Henry had a smile, albeit small, on her angular face. He should be pleased. But he wasn't.

He checked the gold watch as he closed the clasp around his wrist. He'd asked Tiffany and the rest of the staff to show up an hour early. He'd heard the doorbell ring several times so he figured that they had arrived.

Tonight was the last time he would

have to trot out Ally and display her as his wife. He should be relieved. But he wasn't.

Somehow, all the joy seemed to have seeped out of his life with each day that had passed. Even Rod had commented on what a cranky bastard he'd been lately. It was all Ally's fault.

No matter how hard he'd tried to justify her desertion the night they'd made love, it ate at him.

Wasn't he good enough for her? Hadn't her world tilted on its axis the way his had when they'd looked into each other's eyes?

She'd consistently avoided him the next day and the day after. Finally, he got the message that she didn't want to see him. Didn't want to talk with him. Didn't want to even look at him, he guessed. She was running away from him just as she had six years ago. He didn't know why. And that made him crazy.

He'd wanted to talk to her about it. Ask her why she was doing this to him

— to them, but his pride held him in check. She'd broken his heart once before, but that hadn't stopped him from making a fool of himself and falling for her all over again.

He guessed she was spending her days with that damned artist from Dallas. As Burke's mood darkened, everyone seemed to avoid him. Even Tiffany, who was usually immune to anything in the world except business, had stayed away from the office.

Well, for better or worse, tonight was the night. He straightened his tie. Strains of Gershwin reached his ears. The combo he'd hired had begun playing.

'It's show time,' he told his reflection.

★   ★   ★

Burke had just greeted the elder Sakamoto, dressed in a severe black suit, and his son Nishi, the heir-apparent, dressed in expensive Armani. He was talking to Nishi when he noticed the young man's eyes widen with admiration.

Burke glanced over his shoulder to see what had captured Nishi's attention. He felt hot color flood his face. He was going to throttle Ally. Just as soon as he got her alone. How dare she wear something so . . . so totally provocative. She had the attention of every man in the room as she walked toward him.

'Mr. Sakamoto, may I present my wife Ally,' Burke said, linking his arm with hers and pulling her close. That was his undoing. He could smell that perfume of hers. Even her neck looked unbelievably sexy, with tendrils of her soft dark hair artfully brushing against the nape.

With difficulty, he said, 'Ally is an accountant.'

He could feel the heat rising from her flesh even though every inch of skin from her neck to her feet was covered. His body obligingly responded with a heat of its own. He'd never seen a more seductive dress.

Sheer black lace covered her creamy

skin down to a low-cut strapless bodice that held her breasts by some kind of fashion engineering magic. The whole concoction was more erotic than if she'd worn nothing.

Ally murmured a hello in Japanese, with a polite bow no lower than the bow extended her.

The back of the black bodice dipped below her waist, Burke noticed. Sheer black lace covered the expanse of skin from her neck down, making him dizzy with desire.

Burke nearly had a heart attack worrying about the delicate material that held her bountiful breasts. He breathed a sigh of relief when she straightened. The dress had withstood the pressure. He wasn't certain he was going to, though.

'Ah!' Sakamoto smiled. 'How nice to be welcomed in my own language. You speak Japanese?'

'Unfortunately no,' Ally said, 'Although I've always wanted to learn. I had a friend in college who was from Kyoto.

Luckily for me, she spoke English. She's the one who taught me a few words of your expressive language.'

Burke looked at Ally with new respect. She had Sakamoto senior eating out of her hand when Burke had hardly managed to pry a few gruff words of conversation from the man.

Before Burke could do the honors, he introduced Ally to Sakamoto's son. She proceeded to charm Nishi Sakamoto also. The woman was a wonder.

Ally comfortably conversed with Sakamoto. Burke relaxed and began to look for Tiffany. She needed to get involved in the conversation with Sakamoto and his son also. He couldn't see his partner anywhere.

Another wave of guests arrived then. To Burke's consternation, Ally's so-called friend Preston was one of them. Who had invited him? As if he didn't know.

'Ally Cat,' the obnoxious oaf called out. He came over and grabbed her in a bear hug.

For a minute, Burke was afraid her

dress wouldn't pass this last stress test. He unbuttoned his jacket, ready to throw it over her should it prove necessary.

Ally smiled. 'Where have you been, stranger? I saw more of you in Dallas than I have here.'

Burke looked at the man in surprise. If he hadn't been occupying Ally's time, what had she been doing on her excursions in the Jag?

'Hey, Burke, how's it going?' Preston asked, extending his hand.

'Fine, Presley,' Burke answered, gripping the man's hand and squeezing as hard as he could. The artist again gave as good as he got.

Ally turned toward Sakamoto and his son. 'This is my friend Preston Kesey from Dallas. He's an artist whose work appears in several prominent collections in the Southwest,' she said.

'An artist? What medium do you work in, Mr. Kesey?' the younger Sakamoto asked.

'I prefer oil,' Preston answered. He

flexed the fingers of his right hand. 'Though it may be a while before I can hold a brush.'

He and Nishi talked at length about the French Impressionists. After several minutes, Nishi produced a card and handed it to Preston. 'I'd be very interested to see your work. Please call me so we can set up an appointment.'

Surprised, Preston grinned. 'Look forward to it.'

Unwilling to test Burke's forbearance longer, Ally took advantage of a lull in the conversation to excuse herself politely. She took Preston's arm, steering him to another group.

Burke eyed her hands clasped around the man's arm and had to use every ounce of his self-control to keep from separating them.

★   ★   ★

Preston flexed his right hand and wiggled his fingers. 'I'll be glad when you and Burke have your problems worked out,' he said.

'What do you mean?' Ally asked. She looked at him. 'Something wrong with your hand?'

'Yeah, you and your neanderthal husband.'

'He's not my husband, Preston. And you aren't making any sense.'

'Ally, you're so hung up on the man you can't see the forest for the trees.'

'Would you quit talking in clichés and tell me what you mean,' Ally implored.

'Allow me to demonstrate.' Preston pointed at Burke across the room. He seemed engrossed in conversation. 'See the man who's not your husband?'

She nodded.

'Watch,' he commanded as he put his arm around Ally.

To her surprise, Burke's head turned their way. Even from here, she could see the scowl on his face.

'Get the picture?' Preston asked, squeezing her.

'Yes,' she sighed dolefully. 'He's so

jealous of you — with me.'

He shook his head. 'Isn't that what you wanted?'

'I thought it was. But I've decided that jealousy doesn't mean anything in the long run. It just means that someone wants to own you, but they're uncertain of their ownership. I don't want to be owned by him. And I certainly don't want to be used to close a business deal.'

Burke's jealousy hurt. He'd possessed her in the most elemental way, yet he didn't seem to realize that she'd yielded to him because she loved him. He'd used their night of passion to inflate his ego and display his ownership of her to Preston. Couldn't she reach him?

Preston's eyes searched the room. 'Is Tiffany here yet?'

'I don't believe so,' Ally replied absently. 'Preston, if you were the jealous type — '

'Which I'm not,' he said with a grin. 'I guess because I'm more in touch with my feelings than most. Chalk it up to being an artist.'

'But if you were, and you wanted not to be,' she colored, 'what would keep you from getting jealous in the first place?'

He winked at her. 'Self-control.'

She slapped his arm. 'Just answer the question.'

'Okay. The only thing that would help, really, would be knowing you possessed the other person's undying love.'

Ally kissed him on the cheek. 'Thanks, Preston.'

'Ally,' he groaned. 'Are you trying to get my head bashed in?'

★　★　★

Burke saw red when Ally kissed Preston Kesey on the cheek, but he relaxed when he saw Ally leave her friend and circulate to the next group of guests near her. Burke followed the conversation with Sakamoto and his son even as he watched Ally.

She saw that all the guests were introduced around and were given drinks. She excused herself and circulated to the other guests, checking with the caterers occasionally to make sure that food was plentiful and that the drinks flowed freely.

He was filled with pride as he saw how easily she fell into the role of his wife. It was as if they'd given dozens of parties together over the years.

'Your wife is amazing,' Sakamoto said.

'Yes, she is,' Burke said.

Ally was indeed a great hostess, making sure that no guest was alone, and that everyone got a chance to meet everyone else.

'Particularly amazing, given that no one knew she existed,' Nishi added.

'We've been estranged, but that's all over,' Burke said.

'So you have reconciled?' Nishi asked.

Burke looked at him, sensing the

sharp interest that lay behind the polite question. He suddenly realized that his entire future hung in the balance. And not just because of the business deal at hand.

The moment passed as the door opened to another half dozen people. When he saw Tiffany, he was afraid his eyes were playing tricks on him.

'I see Ms. Estes just arrived,' he murmured to the two men, 'Would you excuse me while I fetch her?'

'At least my coat's ready if need be,' Burke muttered as soon as he reached Tiffany.

'What are you talking about?' Tiffany asked, looking around nervously.

'Tiff, what are you doing wearing something like that?' Burke demanded.

'I just thought a business suit would be out of place here,' Tiffany huffed. 'What's wrong with my dress?'

'That's a dress? There's barely enough material in it to qualify as a dress.'

Tiffany's lips trembled. 'Are you

saying I'm not appropriately attired?'

Ally reached them then. She took one look at Burke's thunderstruck expression and the tears welling in Tiffany's huge green eyes.

'Tiffany,' she said, embracing the woman. 'You look lovely tonight.'

'I . . . I do?' Tiffany asked tremulously.

'Yes, you do. Mr. Sakamoto senior and junior are over here. I'm sure they wish to talk with you.'

Burke opened his mouth to say something, but Ally sent him a look that made him rethink his immediate need to speak.

'Why don't we go to the powder room for a moment? Burke can continue keeping the Sakamoto family entertained.'

'Sure,' Burke said. 'No problem. Join us as soon as you can.' He looked at Tiffany again. She did look good. At least she wasn't his woman to have to worry about. 'Uh, Tiff. I was out of line. You do look fantastic tonight.'

'Really, Burke?' she asked anxiously.

'Really.' He smiled as the two women swayed away on their high heeled sandals. He shook his head as he rejoined Mr. Sakamoto. What had come over Tiffany?

'Ms. Estes will join us in a moment. She and my wife had some urgent business,' Burke explained, wondering what the two women were saying to each other.

Ally wished Burke would quit looking at them.

'You're being awfully nice to me,' Tiffany said.

'Well, I'm the hostess with the mostest,' Ally said lightly as they entered the downstairs powder room. She locked the door behind them.

Pulling a tissue from the box, she handed it to Tiffany.

'Thanks.' Tiffany carefully blotted below her eye-lashes. She crumpled the tissue and sighed heavily. 'I guess I should have worn a suit.'

'No. No, you look great. All the men

will mob you as soon as you go back to the party.' She smiled.

'Thanks, Ally.' Tiffany cast her eyes down. 'Would you answer a question for me?'

'I guess. What's the question?'

'How serious is your relationship with — ' She paused and took a deep breath.

'With Burke?' Ally finished. She didn't know how to reply. After all, Tiffany by all rights should be Burke's wife now.

'No! With Preston,' Tiffany said, looking bewildered.

'With Preston?' Ally laughed. 'My goodness! He's a friend. My best friend. Nothing more, Tiffany.'

'But I don't understand the way he acted in the restaurant that night. And Burke said he was your lover.'

Ally had the grace to blush. 'I made it all up, Tiffany.'

'But why would you do something like that?'

'For a million reasons, none of them

very good. I was trying to make Burke jealous — as jealous as I used to be.' She sighed. 'As I still seem to be where that man is concerned. I was jealous of you, Tiffany.'

Tiffany blushed. 'Because of that stunt I pulled at lunch that day, I guess. And then the way I flirted that night in the restaurant. I'm sorry. I don't know what got into me. I was just mad because you had fouled up our wedding.'

'And because I went nuts when I saw you standing next to him in the church. You were marrying my husband. Of course, Burke didn't help matters when he implied that you two were lovers, even though it was a marriage of convenience. So I kind of implied that I had a lover too.'

Tiffany's eyes rounded. 'You're still in love with Burke.'

'Guilty as charged,' Ally said, plopping onto the gold velvet chaise lounge against the wall.

Tiffany sat next to her. 'This is too

funny. You're in love with Burke, so you get Preston to come down here to make Burke jealous. Then I fall in love with Preston, and I'm jealous of you.'

'You're in love with Preston?' Ally squealed. At Tiffany's doleful nod, Ally hugged her. 'But that's great. Preston's wonderful!'

Ally's smile faltered. 'But what about Burke?'

'What about him?' Tiffany asked, checking her hair.

Someone knocked on the door. 'I guess we'd better give someone else the chance to come in,' Ally said, disturbed by Tiffany's casual indifference. She didn't seem to think that Burke would be upset by her defection.

'Let's rejoin the gentlemen,' Ally suggested as they exited the powder room.

'What are you going to do about Burke?' Tiffany asked.

'Do?' Ally asked, thinking that was a strange question. 'Oh, I'll just play the role as best I can. Then I'll go home to

Dallas and get the divorce we agreed on.'

'Oh,' Tiffany said quietly. She studied Ally's bright smile. 'I'm sorry, Ally.'

Ally guided the younger woman toward the Japanese gentlemen.

'There you are,' Burke said, smiling. 'Gentlemen, you know Ms. Estes.'

Tiffany bowed politely and greeted the men. Burke said very little as Ally guided the conversation. She brought out the best in Tiffany, allowing the woman to display her breadth of knowledge about finance. Tiffany discussed facts and figures as easily as some people sang songs.

That is, until Preston wandered over. Tiffany halted in the middle of a word. Eventually, she managed to finish her sentence, but it made little sense to anyone.

Ally smiled, knowing the reason for Tiffany's abrupt loss of vocal skills. She glanced at Preston and noticed that his hand had strayed to Tiffany's back. No one else saw that his fingers traced lazy circles on Tiffany's skin.

Preston chatted a little with Nishi Sakamoto, but Tiffany was left speechless. Ally took pity on the poor girl and said, 'Gentlemen, would you please excuse Ms. Estes, Mr. Kesey, and me?'

To Burke's surprise, the trio walked away. He wanted to follow them, but he couldn't. He quickly lost sight of them as they slipped through the crowd.

Burke lured Dave Hernandez and Craig Bishop into the conversation. Pretty soon he had them talking about a new computer game they'd developed. As soon as the four were engrossed in the conversation, he excused himself and slipped away to find Ally.

15

'I should have known you'd be out here,' Burke said, coming up behind Ally. 'You really love this pool, don't you?'

She smiled over her shoulder at him. 'Yes, I do. It's beautiful here in the moonlight.' She felt a deep sadness. She now knew the truth about love. It didn't truly exist when threatened by jealousy.

She loved Burke. Chances were, she'd never stopped. But she didn't think the same could be said of him. Oh, she suspected that he had loved her six years ago, but she'd damaged that love beyond repair.

'Hello, beautiful.' Burke's lips touched the tender nape of her neck. She trembled in response. The only thing left between them was this undeniable desire.

'Don't,' Ally breathed.

'Why not? You're my wife. I'm your husband. The moonlight is intoxicating.' He kissed her again. 'And I'm crazy for you.'

Ally inhaled sharply. 'We might be husband and wife now, but what about next week when I go home to Dallas?'

Burke froze. 'Go home?'

'Yes,' Ally said, praying he would sweep her into his arms and pledge his love.

Burke resumed his kisses, stringing them up her throat and along her jaw line. His hands swept over her body, tracing the swirls of lace across the tops of her breasts. Surely Ally would relent and stay with him.

'Let's cross that bridge when we come to it,' he said, using all his skill to tantalize her with his hands and his mouth.

Ally shivered. 'But what about our divorce?' She waited for the words she needed. And waited. But the words didn't come.

How could she want that damned

divorce? Especially after what they'd experienced together?

His mouth touched hers lightly. 'Come on, Ally, let's not talk about that now. Can't you feel the magic between us?' He turned her to face him. His hands cupped her bottom and pulled her to him.

'Remember how good it felt that night?' he asked. 'We could slip through the doors over there and be in my bedroom in a second.'

When he kissed her, she didn't resist. Instead, she poured her heart into the kiss. She kissed him as if she'd never stop. His breathing became ragged.

'I want you,' she whispered. 'I need you so much, Burke.'

'And you can have me,' he whispered roughly.

She felt the hard evidence of his desire. He still hadn't said what she needed to hear — what she must hear before she could give herself to him again.

'Burke, please,' she said, intending to

beg him to tell her how he felt.

'I will please you, Ally,' Burke promised. 'I'll please you more than any man ever has.'

Ally's eyes snapped open. 'What did you say?'

'You heard me, sweetheart.' He kissed her hair and then the dimple at the corner of her mouth.

'Only I can pleasure you the way you need.'

His mouth slid down her throat to the tender spot just behind her ear. He kissed her there and then nipped her earlobe lightly with his teeth, making her cry out her need.

'I'll make you cry out in joy like that,' he whispered against her throat. 'Just like the other night. I'll love you so thoroughly that you'll never remember how it was in another man's bed.'

She pushed at him. He stumbled back and fell into one of the deck chairs.

'What?' He looked up. 'What's wrong with you?'

'You're not crazy for me. You're just plain crazy. All you want is this deal to go through. You don't care about me except as something you can own. A toy to keep all to yourself. You have some nerve.'

She was in a towering rage. 'Another man's bed?' She snapped, tapping her foot angrily. 'Why don't you explain that comment?'

Burke cursed beneath his breath, emotionally wrung out and wanting her so much he ached from it. 'I'm not the one who bragged about my conquests,' he parried.

'Back to that again? I didn't brag. And they weren't conquests,' Ally said defensively.

'Right. Let's see, how did you phrase it? Your active social life?'

'Yes, I do have one. That's not the same thing as sleeping with every man in sight.'

He snorted. 'I'll just bet. How many more men do you have sniffing around your skirts in Dallas?'

'You're being obnoxious.' Ally willed the anger to rise. It was so much better than the hurt that waited for her.

'I am, huh? What kind of fun and games do you and your friend Preston indulge in?' Burke seemed bent on lashing out at her. 'What have you been doing with him while you've been hiding from me?'

'You are also being crude,' Ally said.

'I know a hot babe when I see one, and I'm looking at one now. You dressed for seduction in that dress, so don't bother denying it.'

'You're as dense as a fence post.' Ally whirled.

Frustrated at her continued rejection, Burke grabbed her arm. 'I'll be damned if I let you carry on with him under my roof. Don't even think about trying to smuggle him into your bed to satisfy the need I created in you!'

Ally jerked her arm from his grasp. 'Don't come near me again or I'll make sure you can't satisfy any woman for a long while, Burke Winslow!'

Preston and Tiffany stayed huddled in the shadows behind the big oak tree until Burke straightened his clothes and returned to the party. Now was not the time to chase down Ally and offer her comfort. Or to confront Burke and pound some sense into his hard skull.

'I tried to tell Ally,' Tiffany said. She stared up into Preston's eyes.

'Tell her what, love?' Preston kissed the end of her nose.

'That Burke must still be in love with her. Why else would he be using me to make her jealous?'

'How did he do that?'

'Burke and I have never had anything beyond friendship between us, but he suggested to Ally that we were lovers. Think back to the restaurant when you were sitting with Ally. Remember how strangely Burke was acting?'

'Strangely?'

'Yes, whispering to me — laughing with me. True, I was flirting with him, just to get back at Ally. But he'd never acted like that before with me. He was playing up to me just to make her jealous. When all the time, he was only telling me dumb jokes he'd got off the Internet.'

'Jokes? Why, I thought he was saying wicked, sexy things to you.' Preston kissed her eyes closed.

'Burke?' Tiffany's nose wrinkled. 'I'd be surprised if he even thinks about sex.'

'Oh, trust me, he does,' Preston said, kissing her mouth.

★   ★   ★

Ally made it to her bedroom without anyone witnessing her stricken expression. She'd had her second chance, but she hadn't been able to rekindle the love Burke had once felt for her.

With shaking hands, she studied her appearance. Other than being a bit pale, she didn't look like a woman whose heart had broken into pieces.

Maybe maturity brought some kind of acceptance and wisdom, she thought ruefully. At least she'd learned that life did go on. Somehow, you functioned and eventually healed.

She loved Burke. That was a fact, and her feelings for him would never change. But he didn't want her love. He really didn't want to be married to her. Burke only wanted to brand her as his, so he could convince Sakamoto of his stability and trustworthiness.

Perhaps if she didn't fall apart at the seams, she could help him successfully conclude his business deal. She loved him enough to try, although she feared his business would be the only thing that would ever matter to him.

Ally took a deep breath and prepared to give the performance of her life. At least she could give Burke the Sakamoto deal as a parting gift.

16

For the next few hours Ally acted a part that would surely have won her an Academy Award, she thought, pausing for breath.

She had regaled Sakamoto-san and Nishi-san with anecdote after anecdote, all designed to point out the stable relationship she and Burke possessed. Maybe she should write fiction, she thought bitterly, laughing politely at something Nishi said.

The housekeeper came over to consult with her. Ally excused herself and followed Deirdre to the kitchen. From the corner of her eye, she saw Burke approach Sakamoto. Good. Let him take over the playacting, she thought.

'Should we open any more champagne, Mrs. Winslow? It's getting rather late. Everyone should be leaving soon.'

Ally looked at the tub of iced-down bottles. 'Sure. Why not? Open all of them. In fact, I'll have a bottle all my own,' she said.

'Very well,' Deirdre said primly. Evidently she disapproved. Good, Ally thought. Let the drill sergeant disapprove. She didn't care. She waited while the waiter filled a tray of champagne flutes.

'I haven't had a thing to eat or drink tonight,' Ally said. 'So it's time for me to eat, drink, and be merry.' She lifted a glass and handed it to Deirdre. 'Drink up, Mrs. Henry. You're behind. And so am I.'

With that, Ally downed the entire glassful.

Deirdre Henry stared at her aghast. Then to Ally's astonishment, she downed a glassful of her own in the wink of an eye.

Ally whooped with laughter. 'Way to go!' She took two more glasses, ignoring the waiter's warning expression. 'Here, have another.'

When Deirdre raised it and began gulping it, Ally reached out and stopped her. 'Better take that one slower,' she advised.

Deirdre mumbled. 'Yes, you're right. Thank you.'

Ally smiled and patted her on the shoulder. 'My pleasure.' She turned to go then stopped. Turning back she said, 'By the way, you did a great job. This was a quite a party.'

The woman blushed crimson. 'Thank you, Mrs. Winslow. I'm glad you noticed.'

Ally nodded emphatically and left the kitchen. The glass of champagne she'd tossed back had given her a slight buzz. She drained the one she held to keep the feeling going. It felt much better than the icy self-restraint that had permeated her entire being since she'd left Burke on the patio.

She strolled around, still making sure everyone was having a good time. She really should eat something, she thought, but she just wasn't hungry. She lifted another glass of champagne from the waiter's tray and watched as he made his way through the room.

When the waiter reached Burke and Sakamoto, she was gratified to see each of them take a glass. Perhaps they were going to toast their successful deal, she thought, feeling only emptiness at the prospect.

Burke and his guests settled into a quiet corner. She watched and was rewarded to see their faces wreathed in smiles. Suddenly she saw Burke lift his glass in salute to her.

★　★　★

So Ally thought that the only thing he wanted her for was to close this deal? He'd show her how wrong she was.

'My wife is very beautiful, isn't she?' he asked.

'Most beautiful,' Nishi was quick to say.

'There's only one problem,' Burke said. 'She's not really my wife.'

'Your wife is not your wife?' Sakamoto

questioned, sitting straighter.

'Well, she is my wife, but we got divorced. Six years ago. Except she never filed the papers, so we're still actually married.'

Burke felt a huge weight being lifted from his shoulders. If this would win Ally back, then the twenty million dollar gesture would be worth it.

Sakamoto said something in Japanese to his son.

'And you see Miss Estes over there? My business partner?' Burke pointed to where Tiffany stood arm in arm with Preston Kesey.

'Yes,' Sakamoto said, 'A very nice young lady.'

'She and I are engaged.'

'What?' Nishi and Sakamoto asked in unison.

'Well, we were until Ally showed up.'

Furious Japanese flowed back and forth between Sakamoto and his son.

Burke began to relish this destruction of what amounted to a year's negotiation. If you were going to crash and burn, he thought, you might as well do it in a big way.

'And you see the man she's standing with?'

At their nod, he said, 'That's my wife's boyfriend from Dallas.'

'What is this meaning of this?' Sakamoto senior asked, jerking to his feet.

Burke sipped his champagne. Time to get it over with. He was beginning to turn into a pumpkin.

17

Ally said warm farewells to the two Japanese gentlemen. She was grateful that they were finally departing though their rapid-fire Japanese comments — not to mention their strange glances at her — left her puzzled.

After that, the guests began to trickle away in twos and threes. She sighed gratefully when the door closed behind the last one.

'Well, Mrs. Henry,' she said, tiredly, 'as the old song said, 'the shindig is over.''

Deirdre frowned. 'I don't remember those exact words.'

Ally waved her hand airily. 'Different words. Same meanings. I'm going to call it a day. This bottle of champagne and I have a date.' She grabbed a half-full bottle and a glass and headed for the stairs.

Climbing the stairs was as difficult as scaling a mountain, she thought, when at least she reached her bedroom. She stumbled inside and locked the bedroom door. She didn't want to to make it easy, in case her husband decided to start talking about his conjugal rights.

She was exhausted. She peeled her dress off and somehow found the energy to wash the makeup off her face and brush her teeth. But she was simply too tired to shower and shampoo the hair spray out of her upswept hairstyle.

Ally turned back the covers on the bed and crawled in. Then she reached for the bottle of champagne. She'd never swigged champagne straight from the bottle before, she thought, rebelliously tipping the bottle back.

Yuk. It didn't mix well with the taste of toothpaste at all. But it worked great as a sleeping aid, she thought, setting the bottle on the bed table and sliding between the covers. She sighed and in a moment, she was asleep.

★ ★ ★

Sometime, it could have been an hour later or eight hours later, she roused. Something — some noise — had woken her up.

'Ally? Ally, let me in. We need to talk.'

'Talk, schmalk,' she mumbled. She knew what Burke had on his brain and it had nothing to do with talk. She pulled a pillow over her head and shut out his voice.

To her surprise, she awoke at dawn. Golden rays of light slipped through the wood blinds and slanted across her bed.

Ally groaned and sat up in bed, wide awake, but with a headache ferocious enough to bring low the strongest man. Her mouth tasted like the bottom of something she didn't wish to contemplate.

Yet, for reasons unknown, she was as alert and full of energy as if she'd had a restful eight hours of sleep.

Ally stretched, intent on bringing sanity back to her life as soon as possible. She shoved the covers aside and swung her feet to the floor.

She was only a little wobbly as she staggered to the bathroom. Not bad for a woman who'd been up nearly twenty hours without any sustenance other than champagne.

She could do this, she decided, ducking under the shower spray. It was easy. All she had to do was not think about what had happened. She'd think about it tomorrow. That philosophy had served old Scarlett O'Hara rather well.

Of course, not thinking about Burke took some doing, she realized as she prepared to leave. But she'd have plenty of time to master the skill.

She didn't bother taking anything with her except her handbag. With the exception of the dress she wore, which Burke had purchased, she wanted no reminders of the time she'd spent here. It would be easier that way.

Mrs. Henry had been given the morning off so the house was quiet. Ally actually felt regret that she wouldn't have a chance to say goodbye to the old drill sergeant. She'd grown quite fond of the woman, she discovered.

Hurriedly, she penned a note to Burke telling him she would leave the Jag at one of the park and ride lots at the airport, and send him the key she'd used, since he had a spare.

Weakness hit her then. She couldn't walk out without a last look around at his home. She hoped he'd be happy there.

* * *

Burke awoke to the ringing doorbell. He opened his eyes and looked around and discovered he was in his own bed. Damn! He'd wanted to wind up in Ally's bed last night. Though he'd tried to rouse her several times during the wee hours of the morning, she'd ignored him.

The bell rang again and again.

'All right. All right. I'm coming.' Blearily, he focused on trying to get his robe on. Eventually, he managed to stagger to the door and fling it open.

'Tiffany. What do you want?' He blinked against the bright sunlight. 'Do you know what time it is?'

'Why, yes,' she said, looking at her watch. 'It's one in the afternoon.'

That woke him up. 'It is?' How had he slept so late? And where was Ally? The house was ominously quiet.

'I just had to come tell you the news. Nishi Sakamoto just called.'

'Yeah. I'm sorry about that, Tiffany. I'll make it up to you somehow. I know how much you wanted to make that deal work.'

'What are you talking about? They want to sign the papers as soon as we're ready.'

Burke shook his head as if to clear it. 'I'm sorry. Something must be wrong with my ears. I thought you said they went for the deal.'

'They did.' She frowned. 'Although I don't understand their explanation exactly.'

'Why? What did they say?'

'Let me see if I can remember his exact words. Nishi said that his father expected Americans to be highly individualistic, but that you worked too hard at it. But they figured if you could make your personal relationships work, then you could certainly handle any business problems that arose.'

'Does that make any sense?'

Burke laughed. He laughed until he had tears running down his face. 'Yeah. In a weird way, I guess it does.'

'Well, I'll leave you to celebrate with Ally.' Tiffany hesitated, 'By the way, I'm taking a few days off. Thought I'd go to Dallas. Maybe take in some art.'

Burke remembered her and Preston with their arms linked. That made him laugh even harder.

★   ★   ★

He wasn't laughing two hours later as he retrieved his Jaguar from the park and ride lot at Hobby Airport.

'Gee, I'm sorry, Mr. Winslow. I don't

251

know how that scratch got on the hood,' the manager said. 'But I'm sure it was like that when it came in here.'

'Never mind. The car doesn't matter. Just gas it up for me and give me the bill.'

Fifteen minutes later, he was on the Gulf Freeway headed north. If he pushed it, he'd be in Dallas before dark. This time, he'd teach Ally that running away wasn't the answer to their problems.

★ ★ ★

Sighing with relief, Ally opened the door to her apartment. She sniffed. That was odd. She thought she smelled coffee. She tucked the bundle of mail she'd picked up under her arm and tossed her purse on the chair in the small foyer.

Shuffling through the mail, she walked into the living room.

'It's about time you got home,' Burke said.

Ally screamed and threw her mail at him. When she saw who it was, she sagged in relief. Her hand pressed to her chest to keep her heart from racing.

'What are you doing here?' she exclaimed.

'Is that any way to greet your husband?' He stood and walked toward her.

Ally backed away. 'Don't come any closer.' Her relief transformed to sheer panic. Why had he come here? It wasn't fair.

Burke stopped, and he regarded her with amusement. 'Relax, Ally. You and I have some business to discuss.'

'Business!' She said the word as if it were something repugnant. 'I've done all I can to help you with your business, Burke. I can't do any more. I can't be your wife anymore.'

He took another step toward her.

'Don't come any closer. I'll call for Percy. He's just across the hall.'

'You mean Preston,' Burke said, grinning.

'Right. Right,' Ally said, rattled.

'It won't do you any good to call him.'

'It won't?'

'He isn't home. He's still in Houston. How do you think I got your key?'

'I don't know. Just give it back.' She snapped her fingers. 'Right now.'

'I'll be glad to give it to you,' he said, covering the distance between them in two long strides. 'But I'm not talking about any old key. Unless it's the key to my heart.'

Then he was all over her, and she was too swept away to protest.

★　★　★

A long while later, Ally roused. Something was tickling her nose. She opened her eyes and found Burke above her. He was brushing a strand of hair back and forth across the tip of her nose.

'Is this some kind of exotic torture?' she asked, stretching lazily. She loved the way his eyes followed her every languid movement.

'It's time for that talk I mentioned.'

'Oh, Burke, don't spoil things now.'

He shushed her with a kiss. 'No, sweetheart. This won't spoil anything. This will make everything right.'

And it did.

Epilogue

'Hurry, Burke, we're going to be late,' Ally said anxiously.

'If we don't get to the church on time, it won't be my fault. You know how I am about red lingerie.' He grinned at her.

'You are so bad,' she said with a giggle.

'And aren't you glad?' He waggled his eyebrows in an exaggerated leer.

'There it is,' Ally cried.

Burke swung the steering wheel of the Jag. In a maneuver worthy of an action film, he cornered expertly and swooped into the driveway of the church, double-parking the car. 'Come on, Ally, let's hustle.'

They rushed in and dashed to the room reserved for the wedding party.

'We made it,' Ally cried. 'There's my grandmother and your grandfather.

Prepare for a lecture on punctuality.'

Frederick Winslow and Edith Fletcher turned. They both looked anxious.

'I think the only wedding you two have ever made on time was your own,' Frederick grumbled. 'Help me with this darn tie, Burke.'

Ally and Burke exchanged amused glances and began to fulfill their duties as matron of honor and best man.

Before they lined up for the processional, Burke pulled Ally aside. He thanked the powers that be that he'd had a second chance with her for he couldn't imagine life without her.

'How many weddings does this make that we've been to in this church?' he asked, gazing into her eyes.

'Counting our first one and your near second one, and then our reaffirmation of vows, we keep this place in business,' Ally said, laughter sparkling in her happy eyes. 'My favorite part, though, is always when the minister says you can kiss the bride.'

Burke looked over at Frederick and

Edith as they waited for the strains of 'The Wedding March.' The nervous couple were getting a jump on the minister's instructions as they kissed and whispered together.

Ally followed his gaze and smiled at the two people who meant so much to her. Granny Edith had known for months about the unsigned divorce papers. When she'd met Frederick on that cruise and discovered who he was, the two had decided to lend fate a hand.

Without their meddling, she and Burke would never have been brought together in such a dramatic way. She swallowed against the knot of emotion.

'When do you think we should tell them they're going to be great-grand-parents?' Burke whispered, reaching out and stroking her flat stomach.

'Let's wait until the reception,' Ally said. 'In the meantime, we can practice my favorite part of the ritual. Just in case we decide to have another wedding.'

Laughing, he teased her with a chaste kiss on her lips.

'You call that a kiss?' Ally complained. 'Come on, Burke, kiss me like you mean it.'

So Burke kissed her again, this time with all his heart and soul.

'Thank goodness,' Ally gasped, 'some things never change.'

DEAR OBSESSION

I. M. Fresson

Dr. Manley's wife Kate has allowed her son Johnnie to become an obsession, excluding the rest of her family. However, when the doctor takes a new partner, Dr. Paul Quest, everything changes. Johnnie becomes more independent and her husband less willing to go along with her obsession. Kate, now realising that she is in danger of losing her husband, must also accept the bitter truth: that Johnnie is capable of doing without her . . .

ALL TO LOSE

Joyce Johnson

Katie Loveday decides to abandon college to realise her dream of transforming the family home into a country house hotel and spa. With the financial backing of her beloved grandfather the business looks to be a runaway success. But after a tragic accident and the ensuing family squabbles Katie fears she may have to sell her hotel. When she also believes the man she has fallen in love with has designs on her business, the future looks bleak indeed . . .

ERRAND OF LOVE

A. C. Watkins

Jancy Talliman flies halfway around the world to Bungalan, in Australia, to renew an interrupted love affair with Michael Rickwood, who she'd met in London. She remains undaunted on discovering that he's unofficially engaged to Cynthia Meddow, especially given the support of Michael's brother Quentin, and his sister Susan. Jancy settles in a small town nearby. Then as she becomes involved with the townspeople, dam worker Arnulf, and Quentin, Jancy alters the very reason for her long journey south . . .

A NEW BEGINNING

Toni Anders

Rowena had only met her godmother once, so why had Leonora Lawton left Cherry Cottage to her in her will? Should Rowena sell her bequest and continue to run her successful children's nursery, or make a new beginning in the chocolate box cottage two hundred miles away? The antagonism of Kavan Reagan, her attractive neighbour, who had hoped to inherit the cottage himself, only strengthens her resolve to make a new life for herself.